"It's Time For You To Pay The Piper, Mr. Craddock,"

Cordelia said smugly.

"But—but—"

"My father will demand paternity tests. I'm prepared to take you to court to acquire your cooperation. I'm also prepared to pay you for the inconvenience."

"But—but—" His face had gone very pale. Even his voice had lost its verve. "I—I have to know," he said, staring at her with numb shock.

"All right," Cordelia said calmly. "I was visiting Atlantic City just over seven months ago. While I was there, I got what I wanted at the sperm bank you know so well. As you can see, the first attempt was successful."

"But—but—"

"It's true, I'm afraid. You, Mr. Craddock, are the father of my child."

Dear Reader,

When *Man of the Month* began back in 1989, no one knew it would become the reader favorite it is today. Sure, we thought we were on to a good thing. After all, one of the reasons we read romance is for the great heroes! But the program was a *phenomenal* success, and now, over six years later, we are celebrating our 75th *Man of the Month*—and that's something to be proud of.

The very first *Man of the Month* was *Reluctant Father* by Diana Palmer. So who better to write the 75th *Man of the Month* than this wonderful author? In addition, this terrific story, *That Burke Man,* is also part of her LONG, TALL TEXANS series—so it's doubly special.

There are also five more great Desire books this month: *Accidental Bride* by Jackie Merritt; *One Stubborn Cowboy* by Barbara McMahon; *The Pauper and the Pregnant Princess* by Nancy Martin—which begins her OPPOSITES ATTRACT series; *Bedazzled* by Rita Rainville; and *Texas Heat* by Barbara McCauley—which begins her HEARTS OF STONE series.

This March, Desire is certainly the place to be. Enjoy!

Lucia Macro,
Senior Editor

Please address questions and book requests to:
Silhouette Reader Service
U.S.: 3010 Walden Ave., P.O. Box 1325, Buffalo, NY 14269
Canadian: P.O. Box 609, Fort Erie, Ont. L2A 5X3

NANCY MARTIN
THE PAUPER AND THE PREGNANT PRINCESS

SILHOUETTE *Desire*®
Published by Silhouette Books
America's Publisher of Contemporary Romance

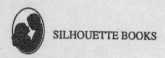

SILHOUETTE BOOKS

ISBN 0-373-05916-7

THE PAUPER AND THE PREGNANT PRINCESS

Copyright © 1995 by Nancy Martin

Printed in U.S.A.

Books by Nancy Martin

Silhouette Desire

Hit Man #461
A Living Legend #522
Showdown #576
Ready, Willing and Abel #590
Looking for Trouble #608
Fortune's Cookie #826
Wish Upon a Starr #858
*The Pauper and the Pregnant Princess #916

*Opposites Attract

Silhouette Intimate Moments

Black Diamonds #60

NANCY MARTIN

has lived in a succession of small towns in Pennsylvania, though she loves to travel to larger cities in this country and abroad to find locations for romance. Now she lives with her husband and two daughters in a house they've restored and are constantly tinkering with.

If Nancy's not sitting at her word processor with a stack of records on the stereo, you might find her cavorting with her children, skiing with her husband or relaxing by the pool. She loves writing romance and has also written as Elissa Curry.

One

"What's the matter, Crash? Your boat spring a leak?"

"Very funny," replied Charles "Crash" Craddock from the folding chair perched on the edge of a New Jersey boardwalk. From that vantage point, with one long, blue-jeaned leg crossed over the other and a can of warm beer balanced on his T-shirted chest, Crash watched his beloved boat *First Love* sink slowly into the Atlantic Ocean with all his worldly goods aboard.

Not that he actually *owned* many worldly goods anymore. He'd sold most everything to keep his deep-sea fishing ventures going just a little longer. But now it looked like the only tourists he might guide would be fishing *First Love* from the sandy bottom.

"What're you gonna do now, Crash?" asked the old man with the fishing rod, standing beside Crash's chair to watch *First Love* wallow deeper and deeper into the swells. A small crowd of regulars had gathered to watch the event—mostly old folks in tattered clothes, homeless people who had come to depend on Crash to bring them sandwiches now and then. The fan club, he called them privately.

The old coot with the fishing rod, Phil, was the only one brave enough to address the owner of the sinking boat. "You gonna deal some blackjack at the casino, maybe? Or flip hamburgers on the Boardwalk and flirt with the waitresses? How are you gonna get along?"

The sad news was that Crash wasn't qualified to do any of those jobs—except maybe flirt with waitresses, which was the only way he managed to eat one vaguely nutritious meal every day and bring a sack of sandwiches to the fan club.

"I don't know what I'll do," he said, taking another morose slug of beer. "Something will turn up."

Something always turned up for Crash. He was lucky that way. Hadn't he won *First Love* in a card game? And hadn't he managed to hang on to his fishing guide job for almost two years? And hadn't he won five hundred dollars in the lottery last winter—just in time to stave off bankruptcy?

Yeah, luck clung to Crash the way body odor clung to lesser men.

But watching *First Love*'s beautiful stern disappear under the surface of the water with a final burplike gurgle, Crash suddenly wondered if maybe the infamous Craddock luck had finally run out. He'd had a string of bad things happen lately. First there had been that little misunderstanding that got him thrown out of Florida waters. Then the New Jersey officials came around asking for a license—a license, of all things! Then that blonde at the casino claimed he'd—well, it was hardly worth mentioning since the whole incident had been a totally trumped-up charge, and the Atlantic City gendarmes had finally seen the light and let him out of jail—although not before he'd gotten into a disagreement over a craps game with a couple of humorless cellmates.

But now this ... the loss of his precious boat. Crash felt as if his dreams were all disappearing before his very eyes. He sighed.

"Uh-oh," the old man beside him suddenly said. "Who's the goon coming in the fancy car, I wonder?"

Crash heard the unmistakable crunch of tires on sand, and Phil began to edge away, saying, "Hey, you don't owe any money to those leg-breakers at the casino, do you, Crash?"

"I owe money to just about anybody who's got a pulse."

"Well," Phil said nervously, "unless you got some spare change in your pocket, son, maybe you ought to take a jump after that boat of yours. Nobody who drives around in a car like *that* is just sight-seeing."

Crash finally worked up the energy to tear his gaze from his sunken boat and glance around at the beach. He saw a long, white limousine roll to a stop just a few yards away. "Who the hell is that?" he muttered.

"I dunno." Phil hastily shouldered his fishing rod. "But I ain't sticking around to find out. You take care of yourself, huh, Crash?"

"Yeah, sure," said Crash, eyeing the limousine with an increasing sense of unease. "See you around, Phil."

The fan club dispersed just as all the doors of the limousine popped open and a platoon of bodybuilders in tight suits stepped out into the morning sunlight. To a man, they wore dark glasses and earphones and sported the thickest necks Crash had ever seen outside a boxing ring—a characteristic that was *not* a good omen. They seemed to be scanning the horizon for enemy submarines.

"Relax, boys," Crash called to them. "The invasion force hasn't arrived yet."

"We'll invasion force you," replied the biggest of the four, arriving on the dock with the kind of muscle-bound waddle characteristic of overly built goons. He had a blond crew cut, a luxurious handlebar mustache and a thick accent—part Arnold Schwarzenegger, part something else Crash couldn't place. Bluntly he demanded, "Your name Craddock?"

"Who wants to know?" Crash rejoined with equal eloquence. During his lifetime, he had spent a surprising amount of time dealing with thugs, and he knew the patter pretty well.

"Shut up and answer the question," Mustache shot back, kicking the chair out from under Crash.

Crash had seen the kick coming—it was an uninspired maneuver and predictable, too. He'd managed to get out of the chair a split second before it collapsed into a mangled mess of aluminum and flimsy plastic. Instinctively, Crash tossed his not-quite-empty beer can at Mustache and turned to make a headlong escape, but the other three guys suddenly had him surrounded, posing in various martial-arts-style positions.

"You guys know how silly you look?" Crash asked.

"We'll show you silly, wiseass," said Mustache, wiping beer from his handlebar and flinging down the empty can. He took a menacing step toward Crash.

"Stop it, Rudi!"

The female voice spoke sharply from inside the limousine, and it had an amazing effect on all four men. They froze in formation, motionless except for a hunting-dog-like quivering, as if they all struggled with their desire to rip Crash limb from limb. Even Rudi, the one with the mustache, was stilled by the commanding voice.

"Rudi?" Crash repeated, amused. "You expect to be taken seriously with a name like Rudi?"

"Enough," said the stern voice. "Behave yourself, Mr. Craddock."

Crash squinted into the darkness of the limousine.

He saw a pair of legs first—a long, slender, shapely pair of legs that started with a pair of feminine sandals and ended with a very short, diaphanous skirt. Then the owner of the legs stepped onto the sand and stood up in the sunlight, removing her sunglasses in a fluid motion, and Crash took his first look at the most devastating woman he'd ever laid eyes on.

She was gorgeous. A tigress, Crash thought at once. Female, but definitely not frail. She looked like the queen of all tigresses, complete with predatory green eyes.

Tall and slim, yet voluptuous at the same time, she had long, gleaming black hair that caressed her bare, golden shoulders and wisped tantalizingly along her patrician cheekbones. Her face was superbly shaped, with arrogantly arching brows, velvet lashes and blazing eyes the color of sunlit emeralds. Her lips were lush and wine-colored—exactly the kind of lips that must make even dying men think of hot French kisses.

And her body! Wrapped in a flowing, delicately flowered pre-Raphaelite dress that was cut low on her breasts and high on her thigh, she caused Crash's own flesh and blood to respond in a rush of lust. He imagined running his hands over those beautiful breasts, those proud shoulders...and that large, pregnant belly.

Crash did a double take and stopped daydreaming. Yep. She was pregnant, all right.

Her otherwise slender beauty made her belly astoundingly prominent, and Crash saw his fantasy evaporate in a shiver of cold reality. She was definitely expecting a baby sometime in the near future.

Funny how he hadn't noticed that right off.

"Uh, maybe you made a wrong turn, lady. The clinic's down two blocks." Crash managed a wolfish grin and jerked his thumb in the direction of town.

She eyed him with a mixture of distaste and hauteur, ignoring his remark and getting directly to business. "Are you Charles Craddock?"

"Depends on who's asking."

Her expression remained aloof and imperious. Her English was impeccable, though ever so slightly tinged with some sort of European accent. "Do you have any identification?"

"'Fraid not. It's three fathoms down by now."

She didn't glance at the sunken boat, but kept her unwavering green eyes trained on Crash with deadly concentration. "You fit the description I have received."

"Oh, is my picture up at the post office, again?"

Rudi took another step and shoved his chin to within two inches of Crash's. "Keep a civil tongue in your head, wiseass, or I'll break your neck in so many pieces—"

"I'll handle this, Rudi," said the young woman. She advanced on Crash in a sexy, long-legged stroll and stopped just a yard away, then sized him up again with a narrowed gaze. Her voice sharpened. "Answer me, please. *Are* you Mr. Craddock?"

Long ago, there had once been a nun in Crash's life, who managed to extract the truth from all the head-strong little boys in her custody by simply fixing her fire-and-brimstone gaze upon the offender and causing him to spill his guts in seconds. All his life, Crash had thought that only Sister Mary Joseph had had that ability. He was surprised to discover that this lovely young woman possessed the same unsettling gift.

"Yes," he said, his subconscious remembering the sting of a wooden ruler slapped on his wrists.

"Mr. Charles Craddock?"

"Most everybody calls me Crash."

"Oh." She frowned beautifully. "Why?"

"Why?" He lifted his shoulders casually. "It's a nickname, that's all."

"Surely nicknames come from somewhere."

"I guess it comes from my habit of crashing every vehicle I've ever owned. I'm not much of a driver, you see."

"Or much of a boat captain, either," she replied, casting a significant glance at what remained of *First Love*.

"You didn't come looking for me just to poke fun, did you, Slim?"

She raised her brows, having heard the edge of ir-ritation in his voice. "Rudi," she said to her minion, "will you take your colleagues back to the car, please? I need a moment alone with Mr. Craddock."

"But, Your Highness—"

Sharply she snapped, "Thank you, Rudi."

Rudi blew an exasperated sigh and signaled his henchmen with a jerk of his head. When the four of them were gathered together again at a discreet spot on the opposite side of the limousine, Crash finally spoke again.

"'Your Highness'? Is that some kind of code name?"

"In a way," she said coolly, "yes."

"I mean, you're not really some kind of— This is America, after all."

She turned away and appeared to study the ocean with detachment. "I'm not an American, Mr. Craddock."

"Then where—?"

"I come from a country called Cordofino. Have you heard of it?"

"I guess so." Dimly, he remembered the name.

She strolled a few yards to a public bench, and Crash followed as if hypnotized. Sitting down was an act she managed to perform with surprising grace, despite her condition, and she crossed her legs demurely. They were wonderful legs, all right. She sat back against the bench and folded her slender arms over her chest. From that position, she looked up at Crash and said, "We are a small European principality, east of France. Our primary industries are winemaking, ski resorts... and gambling."

"Sounds like my kind of place."

"Our wines consistently win international awards. And we have the best casinos in the world."

"'We,'" Crash repeated.

"My father," she said, "is Prince Henri."

"And you're...?"

"Princess Cordelia."

"Yeah." Crash chuckled. "And I'm Elvis Presley."

She accepted his remark seriously. "You don't look like Elvis Presley."

"And *you* don't look like..."

He didn't finish the sentence. For a mad moment, Crash felt like laughing. The chances of European royalty wandering around this particular rundown section of Atlantic City on a sunny morning were almost as likely as the king of rock and roll making an appearance at the local bait shop.

But the laugh caught in Crash's throat, and he took a closer look at the composed young woman sitting before him.

In a heartbeat, he knew she wasn't lying. He *had* seen those high cheekbones and luscious lips before—on the cover of tabloids alongside the faces of rock stars and race car drivers. He caught his balance on the boardwalk fence and stared at her.

She was Princess Cordelia, all right—one of three spoiled princesses who made scenes in nightclubs, threw extravagant birthday parties in foreign lands and gave each other tropical islands for Christmas. They were darlings of the international press—three very photogenic princesses who shared a knack for getting into fashionable trouble at the most newsworthy times. Hadn't one of them recently tried to seduce an English prince in front of a telephoto lens?

Crash shook his head and tried to remember everything he knew about the Cordofinian princesses. Like anyone who'd ever stood in line in a supermarket, he knew Princess Cordelia, Princess Julianna and Princess Angelique were three royal hell-raisers.

But the young lady sitting on the bench didn't look like she'd raised much hell lately. At least not in the last several months.

"Okay," Crash said when he found his voice again. "What gives?"

"What . . . 'gives'?" she repeated.

"Yeah. Where's the hidden camera?" He glanced around. "This *is* a joke, right?"

"No joke."

"Then— How come you're looking for me?" He tried to laugh. "I know I have a few gambling debts, but nothing that's going to concern the Cordofino government."

She studied her fingernails for a long moment. "Do you owe very much money, Mr. Craddock?"

"A little."

"And that's your boat down there, leaking bubbles?"

"Yeah. So what?"

"And you're not exactly dressed for job-hunting, are you?"

Crash rubbed his faded pink T-shirt, which advertised a defunct bar in Key West. "I'm not the job-hunting type, to tell the truth."

"I see. You prefer to let opportunity come knocking, is that right?"

Crash's temper began to simmer. "Stop beating around the bush, Slim."

Her gaze hardened. "You may call me Your Highness."

"Tell me what's going on and we'll see—Slim."

She considered matters and said finally, "I have a proposition for you, Mr. Craddock."

"A proposition? You? For me?" He laughed. "You gonna give me a million bucks or something?"

"If that's what it takes," she said smoothly. "Yes."

Cordelia was gratified to see the cocky American blink his baby blue eyes and swallow hard.

She hadn't come halfway around the world to confront a beach bum with her personal problems, but life in general hadn't been working out for Cordelia lately.

Looking at Charles Craddock, in his torn jeans and tight-fitting T-shirt, she devoutly wished she had never set out on this crazy course of action. It was too humiliating. Too demeaning. But there was no turning back now. Fate had delivered Cordelia into the hands of one blond, sunburned sailor with an appalling American drawl and an even more appalling leer on his playboy mouth.

He was attractive, she had to admit. Tall, lean. An exceptionally well-knit body. His resumé *had* listed a college degree, but he didn't look like a rocket scientist.

There was a certain animal quality to the man, too, that was slightly tantalizing...but somehow made Cordelia's mission harder.

She steeled herself for an unpleasant task. "May I tell you about myself, Mr. Craddock?"

He shrugged and lounged back against a concrete pillar, obviously willing to listen and making no secret that he enjoyed looking at her while she spoke. "A million bucks says you're in charge of this party."

"Thank you," she said dryly. "You know, perhaps, that my sisters and I are the only children of my parents."

"Yeah?"

"I am the oldest, and I stand to inherit my father's holdings when he dies."

"That means you'll be a queen someday?" He whistled and waggled his eyebrows. "Maybe I ought to get your autograph right now, Slim?"

Firmly, Cordelia said, "I will never be a queen. I am a princess and will always remain one, even if I do inherit Cordofino—which is exactly what I plan *not* to do."

His handsome face quirked into a puzzled expression. "Run that by me again."

As plainly as she knew how, Cordelia said, "I don't want to rule a kingdom, Mr. Craddock. I can't imagine any fate worse. So I am doing everything in my power to see that Cordofino goes to someone else—namely, one of my sisters."

"Not great choices, are they?" asked the American. "I mean, isn't there one with a poodle?"

Cordelia withheld a sigh of exasperation. Yes, Angelique constantly traveled with her dog. Actually, she was never seen without Muffin. And, if the truth be told, Angelique was probably not the best choice of a successor to Prince Henri, but Julianna wasn't much better, for she had become obsessed with physical fitness and did little else than jump around her private gymnasium to horridly hard rock music. Neither Angelique nor Julianna was cut out for a lifetime of leadership.

That wasn't Cordelia's problem, however. Her problem was making sure *she* didn't spend the rest of her life suffocating in a palace when there was a whole big, wide world to enjoy.

"The point, Mr. Craddock, is that I'm trying to escape my destiny."

"How come?"

"That doesn't concern you," she said briskly. "I want out, and I'm going to get out. For the past five years, I have refused to marry every prince, count, or archduke my family has scrounged up for me. I won't be a brood mare for the benefit of history!"

The American's wry gaze traveled directly to Cordelia's large belly and remained there for a moment. "Looks like you blew it, Slim."

"This isn't what you think," she retorted defensively, automatically touching one hand to her swollen abdomen. It was an infuriating gesture Cordelia found herself repeating several times a day, and she quickly snatched her hand off the spot. "I have decided," she said, "to spoil myself."

He looked blank. "To what?"

"To make sure no royal family will want me—my own especially."

"And how do you plan to accomplish that?"

"By having a child, you fool!" Cordelia exploded. "Isn't it obvious?"

"It's obvious as hell, Slim. But how do you figure *that*—" he pointed to her belly "—is going to, er, spoil you?"

"It isn't done," she replied, trying to regain her royal composure. "Not in my family. Not for a thousand years has a member of the Halpern family lain with a commoner. My father will be furious. He'll want to disown me. In fact, he's bound by our law to disown me."

"That's what you want?"

"It is," Cordelia said, getting to her feet and starting to pace. She could hardly bring herself to explain the next part of her sordid tale. "The problem is, Father won't take my word for it."

The American began to laugh again. "He doesn't believe you're pregnant? What is he? Blind?"

"It's not the pregnant part he won't believe! I should have realized this long ago, but it's not too late to take care of it. He'll want to see the father of the child with his own eyes. He's like that. You see, if the father turns out to be even remotely royal, I may be forced to remain in Cordofino for the rest of my life."

"So who's the father?"

Cordelia swung on the American and struggled to steady her nerves. "Tell me, Mr. Craddock. Have you always been penniless?"

He snorted. "I thought we were talking about you."

"Are you broke?" she insisted.

"Completely," he said with good cheer.

"And you've been broke before?"

"Frequently. Why, I've been so broke I've actually sold my own blood." He seemed extraordinarily proud of the depths to which he'd sunk. "I can get twenty dollars a pint, you know. And twenty dollars will last me a week, if I'm lucky. Why? Are you thinking of taking up poverty?"

"Besides your blood," Cordelia said, barely fighting back the blush that threatened to ruin her carefully rehearsed confrontation, "is there anything else you've sold, Mr. Craddock?"

His blue gaze clouded over with consternation. "What d'you mean?"

"You mentioned a clinic," Cordelia prompted. "Just a few blocks from this very place. Have you had transactions with that clinic, Mr. Craddock?"

"Now wait a minute," he began, his face turning dark as the whole situation started to make sense. He backed up a step. "What are you getting at?"

"You made a donation of a different kind at this clinic, didn't you?"

"Hold it!"

"You were paid two hundred dollars for your contribution, in fact."

"It was supposed to be anonymous!" An expression of horror spread across his face, and he put up both hands as if to ward off her words. "They promised! No names, no responsibilities—"

"I come from a powerful family, Mr. Craddock. When we ask for information, we get it."

"This wasn't supposed to happen!" he howled.

"It has, Mr. Craddock, and it's time for you to pay the piper, as you Americans say."

"But—but—"

"My father will demand paternity tests. Although I'm prepared to take you to court to acquire your cooperation, if I must. I'm also prepared to pay you for the inconvenience."

"But—but—"

"Yes?"

His face had gone very pale, and he seemed to be hanging on to the fence for dear life. Even his voice lost its verve. "I—I have to know," he said, staring at her with numb shock.

"You want me to say it out loud, Mr. Craddock?"

"Yes," he rasped.

"All right," Cordelia said calmly, "I was visiting Atlantic City just over seven months ago. While I was here, I got what I wanted at the clinic you know so well—I believe it's commonly called a sperm bank. As you can see, the first attempt was successful."

"But—but—"

"It's true, I'm afraid. You, Mr. Craddock, are the father of my child."

TWO

The cold air-conditioning in the princess's private jet finally roused Crash from his state of shock. His first sensible thought was that things were moving way too fast.

"Listen," he said to Princess Cordelia. "Maybe I better think about this for a few days and get back to you."

But she had already unfastened her seat belt and was standing up in the luxurious plane. "Too late," she said heartlessly. "We're already over the Atlantic."

Crash peered out the window of the jet and saw the endless blue expanse of the ocean beneath. Too late, all right. Even too late for a parachute.

What the hell made you do this? he wondered numbly. *The money?*

Not entirely, no. Oh, a million dollars was going to come in very handy, but Crash knew in his gut that the real reason he'd climbed aboard the jet was the woman. She was beautiful. Not just beautiful, but magnetic. And sexy. Oozing sex, in fact. The kind of sex that made a man want to put his hands all over her, no matter how big her belly was.

But even the chance of an erotic one-night stand with Princess Green Eyes was crazy, considering the circumstances. Crash rued the day he'd ever thought of donating future Craddocks to the clinic. What happened to the "Oh, there will be no commitment, sir. None at all"? And what about the "Complete discretion, sir. You'll be anonymous"? And the "Sign here, sir, to waive your rights as a parent. The mother will never know your name."

Crash had never imagined being tracked down by a rich, influential woman with a potentially homicidal father. He leaned his head against the small window and groaned.

"Airsick?" Cordelia inquired. Standing at the sleek mahogany bar, she waited while her bodyguard, Rudi, poured her a glass of mineral water, complete with ice and a slice of lemon. "Or maybe you're not ready to think about fatherhood yet? In either case, I hope you'll have the decency to go to the bathroom if you get worse. I hate being around sick people."

"That's going to change soon."

"You mean this baby?" She took the crystal glass from Rudi without looking at him. "I'm not really worried, Mr. Craddock. Someone else will raise this child."

"That's a relief," Crash said, getting out of his seat, too. So far, the princess didn't seem like the motherly type.

He felt distinctly out of place in the jet's luxurious lounge. The seat cushions were upholstered with a creamy silk that made Crash feel as if he was dirtying them just by getting too close. The matching cream-colored carpet was equally immaculate beneath his salt-crusty deck shoes. The rest of the cabin was appointed with fine wood paneling, brass lamps and low marble tables scattered with fashion magazines, a crystal dish arranged with freshly prepared raw vegetables and a transcontinental telephone. Classy. The whole cabin had the hushed feel of an expensive hotel suite saved for the high rollers—not a maternity ward.

Cordelia asked, "Why is it a relief?"

Still thinking the cabin wouldn't survive ten minutes of occupancy by the average toddler, Crash said, "You're not exactly Mother of the Year material, are you, Slim?"

She sipped her water, continuing to lean against the bar but studying Crash through those beautiful green eyes. "I didn't bring you along for the purpose of listening to your opinions, Mr. Craddock."

"Who's giving an opinion? I'm just making an observation. You're not very motherly."

"And you're fatherly?"

"Hey, I didn't go out and deliberately decide to bring another kid into this world."

"Didn't you? Then precisely what did you expect the clinic to do with your, er, donation, may I ask?" She challenged him with a spirited smile and gracefully raised one eyebrow.

Crash glanced at Rudi for help, but the bodyguard appeared to be entirely oblivious to their conversation. After wiping the already perfectly clean bar with a napkin, Rudi simply stared into space with a neutral expression on his face and his hands clasped behind his back.

"Let's put it this way," Crash said, returning his attention to the princess. "I didn't make the choice to have this particular kid at this particular time. I made my donation, as you call it, thinking I was helping people who really wanted kids."

"And to make a little money for yourself while you performed the good deed, right?" Her green eyes positively twinkled with malice.

Crash sighed. It was his opinion that beautiful women always had a downside. Now, take a woman with a little extra weight around her hips or a nose that hadn't seen a surgeon's knife, and chances were she had a sweet nature and a kind heart. But really good-looking women—especially women who looked as delicious as the princess—they had major problems.

Crash glanced at Rudi again and thought he spotted the ghost of a smug smile as it appeared beneath the bodyguard's full mustache. Clearly, everybody thought Princess Cordelia was the cat's meow.

"I'm curious," Cordelia said suddenly, "tell me one thing."

"You're the boss," Crash replied, collapsing back into his seat.

"Tell me about the money you left with the waitress."

Before he'd agreed to leave the country in the princess's fancy jet, Crash had insisted Her Royal Highness donate her pocket change to a waitress he knew at the Seaside Diner. But he hadn't given the cash to the woman because of some misguided love affair, as the princess no doubt supposed. No, the money was supposed to provide food for Phil and the rest of

Crash's fan club while he was out of town. Crash trusted Josie, the waitress, to take care of the homeless people who'd started to count on him. Cordelia's pocket change had turned out to be nearly a thousand bucks, so Crash had left the country feeling sure Phil and the others would be looked after during his absence.

But for some reason, he didn't want Her Royal Highness to know that.

So Crash said, "I had to cover a gambling debt, that's all."

Oddly enough, that answer seemed to please her enormously. She smiled again—an expression that turned her already lovely face into one of complete perfection. That smile brought Crash's thoughts to a standstill. "I see," she said, obviously delighted at his depravity.

"Make you happy, Slim?"

"That you're a degenerate beach bum? As a matter of fact, I love it, Mr. Craddock. My father is going to be horrified."

"Is that what I'm supposed to do for the million dollars you're giving me? Horrify your father?"

"It will be a snap for you, I'm sure."

Crash eyed her sourly. "Exactly how long do you expect this to take?"

"Why do you ask? Do you have some pressing business with a New Jersey waitress or two?"

"Actually, I just want to know how soon I can start spending my cash."

"In a week or two. Perhaps three. Let's see," she began, counting off the coming events on her fingers. "For starters, we'll need time for the international press to make a fuss—"

Crash felt a pang of disquiet. "International press?"

"Yes, the tabloids, of course. They'll want some pictures of you looking—well, as grubby as possible, I hope. If you could arrange an unpleasant scene or two in a public restaurant, perhaps, or in one of the casinos, that would be nice."

"I'll see what I can do."

"Wonderful. I was also hoping you might insult my mother while you're at it."

"I'd be honored."

She laughed. "See? Isn't this going to be fun?"

"Oh, it ought to be a barrel of laughs, all right," Crash agreed.

"After the press has their field day, we'll have to make sure Papa disowns me."

"Have you figured that part out yet?"

"Oh, I thought I'd play it by ear. Or maybe you'll come up with something spontaneously awful."

"I'll do my best."

"You see, Rudi? This is going to work out fine."

But suddenly her face clouded and she put her hand on her belly. "Ouch."

"What's the matter?"

She sat down abruptly on one of the bar stools, causing her bodyguard to look concerned. "Your Highness?" Rudi asked.

With a frown of pique, she rubbed the offending spot on her protruding stomach. "I never guessed what a nuisance this was going to be."

"A 'nuisance'?" Crash repeated.

"Yes, getting kicked all the time."

"Most women find the experience exciting."

"I'm *not* most women," she replied, setting down her glass. "Royal blood shouldn't really mix with peasantry, I guess. Rudi, I think I'd better lie down for a while. Will you go prepare my bed?"

Her bodyguard moved out from behind the bar. "What about *him*, Your Highness?" He jerked his head in Crash's direction.

"Oh, run along, Rudi," Cordelia said with a smile. "Mr. Craddock couldn't hurt a fly."

For some reason, that remark annoyed Crash intensely. He hated being dismissed as a harmless weenie—a harmless *peasant* weenie. Especially by a smug young lady who obviously enjoyed being in charge. Worse yet, Crash didn't like the bodyguard's proprietary air where the princess was concerned. The two of them acted like an old married couple—and she wore the pants.

Rudi sketched an obsequious bow in her direction. "Very good, Your Highness."

When Rudi was gone, Crash felt a rush of absurd jealousy. "What's he going to do? Turn down the sheets and put a mint on your pillow?"

Cordelia smiled tolerantly. "You don't need to worry about Rudi, Mr. Craddock. He knows his job."

"Does his job involve keeping you happy in bed?"

She stiffened. "What are you suggesting?"

"You know exactly what I'm suggesting. Does good old Rudi play Poke the Princess?"

She drew herself up to the full extent of her royal height and glared down at Crash with all the imperious dignity that could be genetically transmitted through generations of palace living. For a moment she looked like a beautiful, furious goddess capable of hurling lightning bolts down from the heavens.

"I will not be spoken to in this fashion, Mr. Craddock."

"Oh, yeah? How about the way you talk to me, Slim?"

"What do you mean?"

"I didn't come along on this fun ride to get insulted."

"*I'm* the one who's been insulted."

"Oh, go take a nap. You're getting grouchy, and I can see you don't have any idea what I'm talking about. You're completely self-absorbed."

"Mr. Craddock!" she snapped. "Apologize at once or I'll turn this jet around and dump you so fast—"

"Like hell you will," Crash said, getting hot under the collar despite his inner vow to stay cool. It didn't make sense to get angry, but Crash couldn't help himself.

Her green eyes threw furious sparks. "How dare you—"

"Oh, knock it off," he said, and got to his feet. "You can't do a thing to me, and you know it."

"Guess again!" She whirled away and reached for the telephone.

Crash grabbed her arm and pulled Cordelia around to face him. He was delighted to find himself taller than Her Royal Pain In The Butt by a good six inches. "You need me," he taunted. "You need me a hell of a lot."

Her face was sharp with anger, and her eyes blazed. "I can replace you in five seconds, Mr. Craddock. Don't start taking liberties or I'll—"

"You'll what? Have Rudi throw me in the dungeon? Think again, Slim. I'm the one with the all-important DNA. You go looking for my replacement in this scam of yours, and I'll telephone every tabloid you ever heard of."

"That's blackmail!"

"The hell it is. It's called freedom of the press. And I've got truth on my side—provided that *is* my baby you're carrying."

"It is," she spat, standing toe-to-toe, her body rigid against his. "Believe me, now that I've met you, I can see why I threw up for three months!"

"Very funny, Slim. But I've got a feeling this baby's going to teach you more than what it's like to toss your cookies now and then. You've got a lot of lessons in life to learn, Your Royal Rudeness, and I can't think of a better tutor than an infant."

"Let go of me, you oaf!"

"With pleasure."

But Crash suddenly found himself unable to release Cordelia's slender arm. His hold on her kept the princess's body wedged against his, and he could feel the swell of her belly pressed against him.

And inside that belly was a baby—*his* baby. His very own flesh and blood—another Craddock ready to burst into the world. Suddenly it didn't matter who the mother was.

Crash flattened his palm on her belly. He felt heat radiating from Cordelia's skin, but in his mind's eye he imagined the child within. There was a tiny heart beating inside there. A brain that would someday be full of bright ideas and clever schemes. Crash felt his throat tighten at the thought of his own child just waiting for the right moment to be born.

"Wh-what are you doing?" Cordelia said unsteadily, frozen under his touch.

Crash forced himself to look into her face. And suddenly those emerald eyes, that mouth, those gorgeous cheekbones, became more than a collection of perfectly photogenic features. She was lovely, yes, but there was something else lurking behind all that beauty. Crash saw a flash of something startling... something vulnerable.

Something scared.

"Let go of me," she whispered, her voice quivering.

"I will," Crash said, matching her quiet. "But first let's get a few things straight."

"Such as?"

"Such as treating me with a little civility."

"That's going to be hard."

He smiled coolly. "Not as hard as the second thing."

"What's that?" she asked, still suspicious but getting a grip on herself again.

Crash spread his fingers on her belly. "You're going to be good to this baby."

Her mouth opened and it stayed that way.

"You heard me," Crash said. "Either you promise me right here and now that this child gets the best life money can buy, or it's no deal, Slim. I want my son to have a real childhood."

"Your *son?*"

"I may not be the richest man in the world, but I am this baby's father and that goes a long way these days. If you don't promise to be a mother or at least hire the next best thing—and I *don't* mean Rudi—I'll drag you across every talk show, headline and public forum in the world until I make things right."

"Could it be," she asked archly, "the beach bum actually has a conscience?"

He didn't answer that. "Do we have a deal?"

Cordelia swallowed hard. "It's a deal."

As if to punctuate the agreement, the baby suddenly gave a walloping huge kick that blew the air right out of Cordelia's lungs. She reached for the spot but found Crash's hand beneath hers to absorb the impact.

The kick might have sent Cordelia staggering, except for Crash. He wound his arms around her instinctively, drawing her against his chest. Their hands melded over the baby.

Cordelia knew she should resist. But as she blinked up into Crash's stormy gaze, she felt her resistance slip a notch. His embrace was strong, and his body felt lithe and powerful against hers. The pressure of his hand was at once exciting and comforting. In an instant, Cordelia tried to control her reaction, but it was too late. She saw the flicker in Crash's eyes and knew he'd sensed her longing—a longing she didn't fully understand herself. But there it was between them, as obvious as the baby.

She felt Crash draw a ragged breath. He was very still, and Cordelia suddenly feared he might feel the crazy thumping of her heart.

To steady herself, Cordelia rested her other hand on his chest. Maybe she thought of pushing him away, or maybe she simply wanted to touch him. The solid wall of muscle beneath his T-shirt surprised her. Suddenly she wanted to let her fingertips explore further. But she kept her hand where it was and tried to tear her gaze from Crash's intent stare.

His eyes burned through her. His mouth looked hard, yet sensually appealing. She wondered what it would feel like against her own trembling lips.

As if guessing her thought, Crash seemed to draw her closer. Closer by a scant millimeter, that was all.

But it was enough to scare Cordelia out of her wits.

This isn't supposed to happen, her conscience screamed.

She pushed out of his embrace without speaking a word.

Crash didn't say anything. But he hesitated momentarily before he released her and that was enough to communicate his thoughts. He'd considered kissing her, she knew.

Rudi reappeared in the doorway of the cabin at that moment. "Your Highness?"

"Yes, er, yes, Rudi, I'm ready for that nap now." Still shaken, Cordelia straightened her dress and purposefully shook the tangles out of her hair.

"Wait a minute—" Crash began.

Cordelia gathered her wits so that Rudi wouldn't think something odd had taken place in his absence. "I'm sorry, Mr. Craddock," she said in her most princesslike voice. "I'm not feeling one hundred percent at the moment. We'll finish this discussion another time."

As she swept grandly past him, Cordelia heard Crash mutter, "You bet your sweet rear we will, Slim."

With her face turning pink, Cordelia hurried past Rudi, down the hall and into her sleeping cabin. She closed the door hastily—before Rudi could ask if there was anything else she wanted.

Alone, she threw herself across the neatly turned-down bed, wishing she could bury her face in the pillow and scream. But Cordelia's pregnancy had definitely made lying on her stomach a thing of the past, so she contented herself with curling up on one side and squeezing her eyes shut tight.

Kissing a peasant! The idea had actually been appealing! Cordelia shut her eyes and tried to forget the look in his eye when he'd tightened his embrace and nearly pulled her into a long, hard, sexy kiss that might have melted them both into pools of bubbling hot hormones.

Cordelia couldn't blot out the mental picture of Crash touching her belly, either. Nor could she obliterate the weird feelings she'd experienced while he'd held her in his arms and felt the baby kick.

For the first time since she'd been carrying the baby, Cordelia had felt as if there really was a person inside her. A *child*. Not just a pawn in her father's game of life, or a vial full of liquid that the clinic doctor has so routinely planted inside her body eight months ago, but a *living being*.

The enormity of that realization swept over Cordelia like a rogue wave at the ocean. A baby. She was carrying a real baby.

Funny how Crash assumed the baby was a boy.

Cordelia sat up. She had deliberately not let herself think about the baby as a boy or girl. Up until now, it had been a *thing*. But Crash automatically believed there was a little boy inside her.

"Oh, no, you don't," Cordelia said out loud. "You're *not* going to be a boy. I forbid it."

She kicked off her shoes, got off the bed and went to the wall of mirrors that separated her sleeping cabin from her private bathroom. Frowning at her reflection in the mirror, Cordelia decided she didn't *look* any different, but she certainly felt as if something cataclysmic had happened. She struggled for a moment and managed to unzip her dress. Then she removed it and stood there in her bra and panties. She stared at the stretched skin of her belly. There was a *child* in there. Crash Craddock's child.

Slowly she unfastened her bra and let it slip to the floor. Cordelia stared at the rounded weight of her newfound breasts—breasts intended to actually *feed* another human being.

"No way," she said to her reflection. "I draw the line at that."

She hugged her bare breasts, lay back down on the bed and contemplated motherhood.

Nope. She couldn't imagine taking care of a baby. There would be nurses for that. And later, a nanny. Her mother and father had hired a succession of excellent teachers who had overseen Cordelia's upbringing perfectly well. It would be an easy matter to find someone qualified to take care of this child, too. She would put Rudi in charge of hiring the right person.

Relaxed on the bed and cradling her nearly naked body, Cordelia let her mind wander even further afield—all the way to Crash Craddock.

He was awfully annoying, she told herself. So damn sure of himself. Ordering her around. Actually *manhandling* her, too. She remembered the strength of his grip as he'd grabbed her arm. No wonder his child had a kick like a draft horse.

When she'd first hatched the plot to rid herself of the Cordofino throne, it had all sounded very simple.

Get pregnant and prove to Prince Henri that she was ruined forever. Simple, right? but Crash Craddock was not a simple man. In fact, he was starting to seem downright troublesome.

Cordelia caught herself touching her enlarged breasts in a way that made her blush all over again—considering her mind was full of Crash Craddock.

"No, no. I refuse to be attracted to him." Hastily she grabbed the crisp white sheets that Rudi had so carefully smoothed down for her, and she wrapped herself up in them. Then she tried to nap.

It took a long time for sleep to come, however.

In the jet's main cabin, Crash had no such trouble falling asleep. But what his unconscious mind did while his guard was down—that woke Crash up in a sweat.

Rudi glanced up from the newspaper he'd been reading by the twin light of an overhead lamp.

Crash sat up groggily in the half darkness of the cabin. "Sorry. Did I say something?"

Gruffly, Rudi said, "Something about a royal pain in the butt."

"Oh." Crash relaxed once more. "That wasn't so bad."

"Dreaming?" asked Rudi.

"Nightmare," Crash corrected.

With a grunt, the bodyguard went back to his newspaper, leaving Crash to consider the peculiar twists that an unconscious human brain sometimes took.

An erotic dream about Princess Cordelia? Well, some pregnant women were awfully sexy, weren't they? Somehow ripe and voluptuous. Crash had always liked women with a little more flesh on their bones than was currently popular, but he had never really considered the amazingly attractive qualities of a female with child. He could imagine sliding his hands all over those rounded curves, into her secret places, around the fullness of Cordelia's—

"Something bothering you?" Rudi asked, interrupting Crash's reverie.

"What? Oh, no, nothing. Nothing at all."

"You made a noise."

"I did?"

"It sounded like a whimper."

No, not a whimper, Crash decided as he looked out into the inky sky. It had been a growl of determination.

He was going to have her. The princess was going to be his. For one night, at least.

Like an urge for popcorn and beer at a football game, Crash's hunger for the lovely pregnant princess wasn't going to go away. He knew that. It had to be satisfied.

And what did he have to lose? The million dollars was his either way. A night with the princess would be icing on the cake.

Crash settled back into his seat again and closed his eyes, letting his imagination go to work on the right scenario for seduction. Maybe he wasn't cut out for finger bowls and caviar, but Crash knew he was the right man to teach the princess a thing or two about real people.

Three

When the jet touched down at Cordofino's national airport at dawn, Cordelia was pleased to see that Rudi had phoned ahead and alerted the press corps. Peeping out from behind her private cabin's curtains, she noted a phalanx of photographers had taken up battle stations on the tarmac.

"Perfect," she murmured, smiling.

"Thank you, Your Highness."

"Not you, Marcel," she said to the new hairdresser, a high-strung little Frenchman who had been a part of her entourage for just a few months. He had been fussing with her hair ever since she'd summoned him to her cabin along with her dresser, and Cordelia was already annoyed with his darting back and forth to primp her. Fortunately he didn't take offense easily and withdrew to a safe distance to continue frowning at her hair like a frustrated artist.

"Here's your handbag, Your Highness," said Elaine, her dresser. The woman's stone face belied nothing except professional interest as she held out a Chanel shoulder bag selected from Cordelia's traveling wardrobe to exactly match her yellow sharkskin suit.

Cordelia accepted the bag and slipped it over her shoulder. With a critical glance into the mirror, she nodded once. She rarely fussed over dressing. That was what she paid Elaine to do, and as a result, Cordelia managed to land on a number of best-dressed lists every year. Thank heaven Elaine had found a selection of high quality maternity clothes in time for Cordelia's return to her homeland. Cordelia had spent the past several months wearing sweat suits while growing bigger and bigger in the privacy of her family's summer estate in the Carribean. Clothes hadn't mattered then.

But today Cordelia found herself wondering what Crash would think of her carefully selected outfit. Would he like the yellow color? Would he appreciate the precise buttons and severe cut? Or was he the kind of man who preferred women in floaty, romantic clothes? *Damn, but I wish I had my figure back.*

Stop it, she ordered her imagination. *Stop thinking about that man. He'll be out of your life in a week or two.*

She turned away from the mirror and said curtly, "Let's go."

The trio exited the cabin with military precision.

In the jet's lounge, Cordelia came upon Crash, who looked even more worse for the wear after sleeping in his seat during the flight. His hair was squished on one side, and he had obviously just awakened. Still, he managed to look as virile as a panther waking from a jungle snooze. Cordelia felt her heartbeat accelerate.

"Are we there yet?" he asked with a sleepy grin.

"We're definitely here, Mr. Craddock. And it's time for you to start earning your paycheck."

Crash blinked at Cordelia. "Wow. You look great."

"Hmm. Thank you." Cordelia fought down a blush. Why should a simple compliment from a bumpkin make her feel as if she was back at finishing school again? Her suit made Cordelia feel like a Volkswagen. But judging by his stare, Crash didn't seem to notice her pregnancy.

She hoped the press would be more observant.

"Well, what's going on?" Crash asked, wiping one hand down his bleary face as if to clear his thoughts.

"We've landed in Cordofino. And we're about to meet the press."

"The press?"

Marcel had begun to flap his hands wildly while staring at Crash with a horrified expression. "Your Highness," he pleaded. "Give me an hour to cut this—this man's hair! And shaving is an absolute necessity! And his clothes! *Mon Dieu!* He is a ruffian!"

"Who the hell are you?" Crash demanded, glaring down at the little Frenchman as if he were an annoying terrier complete with a bristling mustache and infuriating yap.

"My hairdresser," Cordelia replied to Crash. Turning slightly toward Marcel, she coolly assured him, "This man is nothing for you to worry about, Marcel."

Crash ignored her slight and gave her one of his sly grins. "You can't comb your own hair?"

"I have more important matters to attend," Cordelia said crisply. "Marcel, that will be all. You and Elaine may take the second car to the palace."

"But—but—" Marcel's face was purple with anxiety. "Your Highness isn't going to be seen in *public* with this man?"

"Yes, I am." Cordelia's voice turned to steel. "Dismissed!"

Elaine knew her business, and her stoic face didn't change as she shepherded the apoplectic Marcel out of the main cabin and back into the servants' section of the jet.

Crash was amused. "Do you plan to have him whipped for insubordination later?"

"I don't need your advice, Mr. Craddock. I have managed my own household since I was thirteen."

"Looks like you haven't changed your management style since then."

Cordelia tried to give him a withering look. "I know how to handle them. This way."

Rudi wrestled open the jet's door, and the official gangway was wheeled out from the airport's small terminal. Rudi preceded Cordelia out the doorway and descended the steps quickly to make a path for her through the crowd that immediately gathered at the bottom of the stairs.

"Wow," said Crash as he stepped into the open doorway of the jet. He squinted against the blinding alpine sunrise. "I guess this is the royal welcome."

The crowd gave a collective gasp when Cordelia made her appearance beside Crash in the doorway. Then the flashbulbs began to explode like fireworks. She saw photographers jostling for the best angles and knew they were getting their first real pictures of the royal pregnancy. She heard shouted questions from the mob of about two hundred people—a crowd at least twice as large as she usually encountered at the Cordofino airport. Rudi had done a good job of advance work.

"Your Highness! Your Highness!" One especially determined reporter jumped up and down to get her attention. "Are you married? Did you elope in secret? Is this your Prince Charming?"

Cordelia plastered a smile on her face and hoped it didn't look as terrified as she felt. She waved to the crowd with one hand and wound the other through Crash's arm as if he was indeed her Prince Charming. "It's so nice to be home!" she called back.

"You're not answering their questions," Crash murmured out the side of his mouth. "Do you mean to tell me that nobody knows about this pregnancy scam of yours?"

"Just be quiet and wave," she said sotto voce. "Try to look respectable."

"I thought the whole idea was that I'm *not* respectable."

"You're right. Go ahead and look natural."

"Very funny."

"God, it's hot. Are you hot?"

"No. It's actually quite pleasant. What's the matter? You're not feeling well?"

"I'm fine. Let's go."

Cordelia started down the steps, hanging tightly on to Crash's arm and doggedly keeping her smile in place for the benefit of the cameras. She was surprised by the sudden rush of heat from the tarmac. Cordofino wasn't usually this hot so early in the day.

Tilting her face up to Crash in case the evening newspapers needed a loverlike pose for their next front page, she asked, "Would you mind punching a photographer? Just to establish your awfulness right away?"

Crash continued to glower suspiciously at the crowd. "I'm a nonviolent man, Slim. My contract doesn't say anything about fisticuffs."

"One punch?"

"Forget it."

"A little kick?"

"Bloodthirsty, aren't you? No, they'll just have to look at me and draw their own conclusions for the time being. Are you sure this is safe? I don't think Rudi can handle this bunch."

"Of course it's safe. Listen, I'll throw in a bonus," she wheedled. "A thousand dollars for a punch. Two if you break a camera."

As it turned out, she needn't have offered the extra money. When they reached the last step, the crowd suddenly swarmed closer—everybody shouting questions and taking pictures in a frenzy of excitement. Rudi was swept back against the gangway and nearly fell, despite his size, and for a split second Cordelia feared she might have miscalculated the scene. Suddenly there were too many people, all wanting to know the story she'd kept secret for months.

Crash cursed under his breath and quickly put himself between Cordelia and the nearest reporters. She started to back up the steps, but stumbled and cried out.

"Get back, damn you!" she heard Crash shout at the reporters. "Rudi, do your job for God's sake!"

Crash's instinctive reaction to protect Cordelia gave Rudi a split second to regain his feet, and suddenly the two men began to work together. Forming a flying wedge, they forced their way into the crowd, with Crash pulling Cordelia along by her wrist behind him. They reached the terminal in just a few steps, but Cordelia felt herself shoved from all sides as they pulled her through the double doors. She stumbled again, feeling dizzy in the heat.

"Crash," she called, without thinking. A wave of blackness had begun to swell up around her like some kind of hot, nightmarish undertow.

"Uh-oh," said Crash as he glanced back at her. Their eyes met despite the confusion, and the power of his gaze had an even queerer effect on Cordelia. She felt her knees weaken. Without hesitation, Crash returned to her side. "What's wrong?"

"I think... I think—"

"Oh, hell, don't faint, Slim. Not here."

But she couldn't control what was happening. Crash swept Cordelia off her feet with strong arms and carried her bodily through the doors. She didn't remember anything else.

In the royal family's antique Rolls-Royce limousine a few minutes later, Cordelia's head cleared gradually. Finally she sat up in the back seat and pressed her palms to her cheeks. "You didn't have to do that, you know."

Crash raked back his hair as the car gathered speed. He looked angry and shaky. "I knew that place wasn't secure. You could have gotten knocked over. And in your condition— I didn't have to do what?"

"The gallant prince act," Cordelia replied, flustered at finding herself so weak. "You're not getting a bonus for carrying me out of there."

"Are you kidding? It was perfect." In a flash, he regained his easy calm. Making himself at home in the elegant car, Crash leaned forward and grabbed a small bottle of mineral water out of the refrigerator. He twisted off the cap with one effortless jerk. "I guarantee we'll be on 'Entertainment Tonight' in a few hours, bouncing off satellites worldwide."

"A little local publicity was all I wanted."

"International publicity will get the job done faster." He extended the open bottle to her. "Feel okay now?"

"I'm fine!"

"Take this anyway." Crash pushed the bottle into her hand.

Cordelia accepted the bottle unwillingly. For some reason, it was easier to be rude to Crash than admit one near-kiss had changed anything between them.

Crash didn't seem to notice her state of mind and leaned forward to rummage in the refrigerator again. He said, "You wanted to make a splash, right?"

"I wanted to make a *point,* not a splash," Cordelia retorted, sliding into the farthest corner of the Rolls. He didn't understand at all. What Crash had seen at the airport was exactly the kind of hullabaloo Cordelia wanted to escape. Permanently. She hated being watched all the time. Photographers who popped out of hotel bathrooms to snap her picture were the bane of her existence.

Crash dug another bottle out of the refrigerator, then slid open the glass partition between the front and back seats. He passed the bottle of mineral water through to Rudi who, looking hot and angry, was sitting beside the driver. Rudi accepted the bottle without a word, and Crash slid the partition closed once more.

Then Crash looked at the princess as she sipped the water. She was shaken up, he noted, but too proud to admit it. Pale, she slumped against the car's plush upholstery. For an odd instant Crash was tempted to hold her hand, maybe put his arm around her shoulders. She looked like she needed a friend at that moment.

"You okay?" he asked.

She stiffened, collecting herself. "Of course I'm okay. Stop asking. You're not my governess."

She was back to normal—a haughty little snob with her pointed nose elevated as she turned her face to the window. *What gave you the idea she might be a human being under that princess routine?* he wondered.

Suppressing a grunt of disgust at his own foolish ideas, Crash glowered out the other window and got his first look at Cordofino.

It was a damn beautiful place, he thought grudgingly as the Rolls Royce swooped along the cobblestoned streets of the city. The morning sunlight poured molten gold over the ornate buildings—all of which seemed to have been built by the same French architects who had built the oldest sections of cities like Paris and Leningrad. Every second-floor window had a balcony cascading with geraniums. Every street corner seemed to be occupied by white, horse-drawn carriages waiting to take tourists for romantic rides around the city. In a beautifully tree-lined park, Crash caught a glimpse of two uniformed nannies wheeling matching white wicker baby carriages along a yew-lined avenue.

The Rolls flew over a humpbacked bridge, showing Crash a flash of silver—a serpentine river, complete with glowing lamps, a lighted tourist barge and curling mist.

And above the city towered the Alps. The glittering sun turned the snowcapped summits to a storybook pink.

The whole place looked like something out of a fairy tale.

"Pretty," Crash said out loud.

"We can afford it," Cordelia replied coolly. "Cordofino is one of the wealthiest principalities in the world, thanks to our casinos. We have more than enough money to keep our country looking like a resort."

"Which keeps the tourists coming."

She shrugged. "Tourism is our primary source of income. Other countries worry about feeding their poor, employing their population, keeping their food and water supplies clean. We've done all that. Now my father's job is making rich people happy at the roulette tables."

"Sounds like a pretty good life to me."

"I imagine the life of a garbage collector sounds good to you."

Crash gritted his teeth. *It's going to be a long couple of weeks if you let her get under your skin all the time,* he told himself quickly. He couldn't refrain from asking, "What's the matter? Are you scared now that you're so close to confronting Mom and Dad?"

Her head snapped around. "Of course not!"

"They don't have a clue, do they? That you're pregnant? How did you manage to keep it a secret this long?"

"I—I—"

"You might as well tell me everything, considering I'm supposed to be the kid's father. Hell, I *am* the kid's father, so I ought to know a little something about his conception. What are you planning to tell everyone? The truth?"

"No! That would spoil everything."

" 'Spoil everything'?" Crash repeated.

Her color seemed to heighten, and she avoided his gaze. "Technically, I'm still, er, pure. I've never actually, I mean, you and I—we haven't—"

Crash laughed. "I get it. So what? You're obviously pregnant or you're keeping a mighty ripe watermelon in there. Who's going to know the way it really happened?"

"Everyone."

"Everyone?"

"That's what I said," Cordelia snapped. "I have servants around me every moment—waking as well as sleeping. In many respects, I don't live in the twenty-first century."

Crash frowned. "What does that mean? Your handmaiden is supposed to carry the bloody sheets to your father as proof of your lost virginity?"

"Well," she said uncomfortably. "Yes. That's exactly what's supposed to happen."

Crash took a moment to digest that information, and then he laughed incredulously. "Do you mean to say you're a *virgin?* With that stomach? I love it!"

"I hope," Cordelia said coldly, "that you'll keep your affection for this situation a complete secret. I'm paying for your cooperation, Mr. Craddock. Please."

"Please? Okay, okay," he said, still amused. "What do you want me to say?"

"There isn't time to explain now," she said, looking out the car window. "Just follow my lead."

"Whatever you say, Slim."

"And stop calling me Slim!"

She *was* nervous, Crash decided. He liked her off balance like this.

The car slid through a set of medieval iron gates that were guarded by stone lions. The gate—electronically controlled from a guard tower that sat discreetly behind a stone pillar—automatically swung shut after the car. Crash noted that the royal family didn't spare the expense for state-of-the-art security equipment when it came to guarding the castle.

And it was a castle, all right—a regular storybook illustration, complete with gaily uniformed guards, flags waving atop the turrets and a huge, chain-operated drawbridge.

The chauffeur drove the long car across the drawbridge and carefully maneuvered it to a stop under a green-and-white striped canopy. From inside the castle came a bustle of servants—all in crisp navy-and-white livery. They formed two lines at the door as one very tall, elderly gentleman in white tie and tails solemnly approached the car, looking like a stork with sore feet.

"Who's this?" Crash asked. "Lurch?"

"His name is Fenwick," Cordelia replied. "He's Master of the Household—has been for thirty-three years."

Fenwick opened the car door with one white-gloved hand and bowed deeply. In a voice that was a dead ringer for that of Vincent Price, he said, "Welcome home, Your Highness."

"Hello, Fenwick." Cordelia stepped out of the car. "Is His Majesty at home?"

Still bowing and therefore unaware of Cordelia's physical shape, Fenwick said, "Yes, Your Highness. In the morning salon."

"Good." Cordelia swept past the rest of the goggle-eyed servants and into the castle.

As she disappeared, Crash got out of the car and put out a handshake to Fenwick, who was still bowing. *Maybe he's got a bad back,* Crash thought. He clapped the old man on the shoulder and said heartily, "Hey, there, Fenwick. Glad to meet you. I'm Crash. Crash Craddock."

The sound of Crash's American twang prompted Fenwick to forget about bowing. The old man straightened in astonishment, and his rheumy eyes bulged as he absorbed Crash's T-shirt, jeans and run-down shoes. He was speechless.

Rudi came up behind Crash and grabbed his arm roughly, saying, "This way, Craddock."

Giving a grin and a roguish wink to the collection of very pretty parlor maids flanking the door, Crash followed Rudi into the castle.

Cordelia had gone on ahead, giving Crash time to look around.

And he looked, all right.

The home of the Cordofino royal family began with a two-story rotunda complete with marble floor, gilded walls, two crystal chandeliers straight out of *Phantom of the Opera* and vaulted ceiling liberally painted with cavorting cherubs. A thick red carpet led to a double staircase. Crash approached the staircase slowly, still staring around himself in wonder. The stair treads were mirrors.

"Not bad," Crash said to Rudi. "Who joined forces to design this place? Pope Paul and Liberace?"

Rudi jerked his head up the stairs. "Get going."

Before Crash could obey, the enormous chamber suddenly echoed with a blood-curdling scream.

Rudi and Crash exchanged a glance, then vaulted up the stairs two at a time.

The red carpet went about a quarter of a mile down a corridor, straight to a set of doors big enough for a fire truck to drive through. The doors opened into a room the size of an Olympic stadium that was decorated with several million yards of red velvet and a bunch of gilt furniture probably named after some dead French king. The walls were covered with enough swords and guns to mount a global war. There was even a cannon in one corner.

Crash and Rudi skidded to a stop, shoulder-to-shoulder and breathing hard.

In the middle of the floor lay a woman who was either dead or had fainted. She was dressed, Crash noted, in enough jewelry to start a pawn shop. Over her prone body stood Cordelia and the man who had to be her father, Prince Henri of Cordofino. He was tall, handsome, completely bald and just as volatile as Cordelia. They were shouting.

"How could you do something so reckless!" the prince thundered in a voice loud enough to be heard in Austria.

"You drove me to it! You *and* Mama!"

"You are completely irresponsible! You'll never be fit to govern this country!"

"I've been trying to tell you that all my life!"

"I forbid you," shouted His Majesty, "to deliver this child!"

Cordelia threw back her head and laughed. "Even *you* don't have the power to stop a baby, Papa! Relax and enjoy it—you're going to be a grandfather very soon!"

"How dare you keep this information from us!"

"My body is my own business!"

"Not in this country, it isn't! You have royal blood in your veins, young lady, and I won't see it polluted by—"

"Oh, give it a rest, Papa! I'm pregnant and you can't do a thing to stop me now!"

The prince's bald head and smooth face were perfectly suntanned, as befitted a man who spent nearly all his waking hours on a tennis court. But underneath the tan, his flesh was dark with rage. "And who, may I ask, is the father of this child?"

Cordelia stepped back with all the melodramatic flair of a bullfighter and indicated Crash with a sweep of her arm. "Papa," she said sweetly, "I'd like you to meet Crash. Crash Craddock."

"A—a—?"

"Yes," said Cordelia, sounding triumphant. "He's a commoner."

Crash put his arm around Cordelia and saluted cheerily. "Hiya, Your Highness."

The prince looked him up and down and finally skewered Crash with a glare that might have slaughtered a lesser man. He turned even more purple at the sight of Crash's faded clothes and unshaven face.

"No," he said hoarsely, trembling with fury. "I won't have it!"

"Papa," Cordelia warned. "Your blood pressure—"

"Yeah, take it easy, Pop." For dramatic effect, he gave Cordelia's cheek a quick nuzzle and kiss. "We want you around to help christen Junior." He patted Cordelia's belly with feigned affection.

"Do you mean to tell me," the prince growled, "that you and this man—that you actually—"

"We're having a child together, Papa."

"When did this...this abominable act take place?"

"No twenty-four-hour surveillance is flawless, Papa. Your henchmen can't keep me under lock and key."

"But—but I can't believe—"

"Trust us, Pop," Crash put in. "We did the dirty deed and now your little girl's got a bun in the oven."

"A bun— I won't have it!" the prince bellowed. "I won't, I won't, I won't!"

Then he snapped. Prince Henri leapt over his wife and seized the first weapon he could lay his hand on— a sword inlaid with rubies and mother-of-pearl that sported a blade about two yards long. Yanking it off the wall with all his strength and lifting the sword over his head, the prince let loose a hideous battle cry and launched himself upon Crash.

"Papa! Don't you dare! Guards! Rudi! Stop him!"

Crash always prided himself on knowing when to fold his cards. He fled.

Four

Cordelia's search of the palace ended half an hour later when she found Crash safe and sound in a closet.

She threw open the door and found him quite comfortable as he sat cross-legged on the carpeted floor of her own extensive wardrobe, counting shoes. "What do you think you're doing?" she demanded.

Crash looked up calmly from a purple velvet pump he'd been turning over in his hand. "Do you know there are three more pairs of shoes exactly like this? And they're all ugly! It's amazing what some women will buy!"

"Give me that!" She snatched the shoe out of his grasp. It had been a gift from her spendthrift mother—along with the other matching pairs, but now wasn't a good time to go into long explanations. "Have you been pawing through all my clothes?"

"No, I've only pawed through the shoes." Crash remained unruffled by her anger, and he gave Cordelia's legs a long, appreciative glance. "How's your pop? Is he still on the warpath?"

"Yes, thanks to you."

He heard the note of exasperation in her voice and lifted one eyebrow. "That's what you wanted, right?"

"Of course it is." Cordelia pulled herself together. "You were obnoxious, and he was horrified. I just— I guess I didn't expect you to be such a good actor."

He had a boyishly naughty grin. "Who says I was acting?"

Cordelia couldn't stop a wry smile of her own. "My mistake."

"Everybody makes 'em now and then," he said with a self-deprecating shrug. "Like me a few minutes ago. There were two little blue-haired ladies in here when I arrived. They went into hysterics—something about violating the purity of this room or something—and nothing I said would calm them down. I offered to take a shower, if that would help, but—"

"They were probably Ida and Ada."

"Who?"

"My Ladies of the Bedchamber."

"Are those something like elderly bridesmaids?"

"Not exactly, no. They're rather like secretaries and housekeepers and—well, they were my nannies when I was little, and they were both in their sixties then. You shouldn't have frightened them. They both have heart conditions."

"They seemed pretty healthy to me when they ran out of here. I figured they were on their way back with a couple of double-barreled shotguns, so I closed the door and camped out in the dark."

Cordelia held back a laugh at the thought of Crash cowering before Ida and Ada, two faint-hearted, blue-blooded Cordofinian ladies who were both in their eighties. "Well, I'm sure it's safe to come out now. Care to risk it?"

"As long as you're here to protect me."

"Come on." She tossed the purple shoe back into the closet, turned away and walked across the expanse of her bedroom to the enormous pink-canopied bed that had been hers since childhood.

Crash uncoiled his long legs and got up. He followed her out of the closet and ambled into the bedroom. "Rudi said I should hide in here. He seemed to think your old man wouldn't be caught dead in this wing of the castle."

"You're right, he wouldn't. This wing is for my sisters and myself. He's busily having a temper tantrum in the north wing, anyway, so you're safe."

"Where's the north wing?"

"About half a mile from here."

"What a relief. He'll have to hire a cab to find me." Crash strolled past Cordelia's set of matched suitcases, which had been brought upstairs already. Beside her cases lay the rumpled duffel bag they'd hastily purchased at the airport and filled with a few necessary items for Crash.

Then he looked around and saw Cordelia staring at the duffel bag, too.

Amused, he moseyed over to the bed, his hands loosely thrust into his jeans' pockets. He eyed her for a moment as she sat stiffly on the bedspread. "Having second thoughts?" he asked.

"No!" She shook her head determinedly. "More than ever I'm convinced I'd hate spending the rest of my life in this palace."

"What's the problem, then?"

"Problem?" Her voice was too high and sounded strangled, but Cordelia couldn't do anything about that. "I don't have a problem."

"You're tense as a bowstring."

"I am not."

"You are, and I can prove it." Crash suddenly knelt down on one knee and began tugging off Cordelia's shoes one at a time.

She tried to yank her foot from his grasp. "What are you doing?"

"What does it look like? Making you comfortable."

Cordelia looked archly down at him. "Worried that I'm not taking good care of your baby?"

"Maybe. There—feel better?"

He had removed both her shoes and proceeded to gently massage one stockinged foot between his two strong hands. To be honest, it felt heavenly. Cordelia nodded. "Y-yes."

"Good." He went on massaging and glanced around the large suite at the same time. "So this is your apartment, huh? Cozy little football stadium, isn't it?"

Cordelia had to admit her palace penthouse probably looked gigantic to the average eye. The canopied bed took up an octagonally shaped alcove that connected on one side to the dressing room and a bathroom with a Jacuzzi big enough to accommodate eight people. Through an opposite set of double doors lay her own dining room with a table capable of seating

twelve for dinner, her office with a genuine Louis XVI
desk and the latest high-tech computer money could
buy, as well as a gracious book-cluttered sitting room
that contained a fireplace and a French window over-
looking all of Cordofino. The window led to the ter-
race and the glassed-in gazebo that housed her private
swimming pool.

This wing of the palace also contained equally
comfortable quarters for Cordelia's two sisters, not to
mention enough staff members to handle the house-
keeping tasks, plus their private gymnasium, a movie
screening theater, an industrial-size kitchen and the
billiards room that—in a rare economical use of
space—also doubled as a library.

The furnishings in the whole wing were plush and
feminine. Cordelia and her sisters had seen to that.
The fabrics on both furniture and windows were
mostly pink and white chintzes, the carpets immaculate powder blue. Every lamp, table and candlestick
had been carefully selected by one of the princesses to
reflect their gender and feminine taste. Fresh flowers
were changed daily by the staff. The paintings were all
Impressionist works by noted artists, both dead and
alive. Antique crystal bowls of scented flower petals
stood on strategic tables. The final result was bower-
like.

Most men would probably feel weird in such lushly
decorated rooms.

But Crash didn't seem fazed by all the frippery,
Cordelia decided. In fact, the feminine nature of her
living quarters simply made him appear more mascu-
line than ever before.

It was damned disconcerting.

With his expert hands rapidly turning her feet into warm jelly, Cordelia felt her whole body start to relax. "Look," she protested, though without putting her heart into the words, "you really don't have to do that."

Crash's flickering gaze met hers. "But you're enjoying it."

"Since when do you care about my enjoyment? I offered you a purely business arrangement—"

"Who says we can't enjoy the business?"

"Now, wait a minute," Cordelia began, again trying not too hard to pull her foot out of his insistent grasp.

"Take it easy. You've had a rough day." He continued the exquisitely sensual massage up Cordelia's slim ankles to her calf muscles. "And I haven't done much to earn my million dollars yet—except act like a jerk."

"Which seemed to come quite naturally," Cordelia observed wryly.

He didn't take offense. "There are a few other things I do pretty naturally, too."

"Do I really want to know what those are?"

"I think you could guess," he said softly, smiling. "But then, considering your lack of experience, maybe you can't."

"Mr. Craddock—"

"Call me Crash. That's my name. Say it."

His hands were magical, Cordelia thought. Instinctively they seemed to find every tense nerve-ending in her legs, then work gently to ease the tension.

"Crash..." she began unsteadily, "I don't know what you're up to, but..."

"Yes?"

"I—I must admit it feels pretty good."

He smiled into her eyes. "I worked as a masseur for a while—nothing formal, just a way to pick up a few bucks. If you want to take off all your clothes, I could make you feel even better."

"No, thanks," Cordelia said, smiling but finally working up the effort to pull out of his grasp. Being alone with him in her bedroom had an odd effect on her. She felt a flutter of anxiety inside—and also a twinge of pleasure that seemed very wicked indeed. "I think this has gone far enough."

"Too bad," Crash murmured, one hand lingering on her knee.

In another instant, his hand might have crept over her knee and up the length of her thigh. Cordelia almost willed it to happen. His touch was silky soft, and pinpoints of excitement prickled on her skin. She could imagine how sensual his caresses might feel, how they'd lull her further into a state of delicious languor.

Unconsciously, Cordelia began to lean down toward Crash. His mouth looked wonderfully sexy. As if drawn by a powerful magnet, he began to arch toward her, too.

It would have been a delicious kiss. A quiet, unhurried, erotic kiss there on the satin bedspread.

But at that moment they were interrupted by a strident voice saying, "Yes, it's very bad!"

They sprang apart. On a gasp, Cordelia turned to see her mother, Princess Geraldine, come sailing through the bedroom door. Her red brocade dressing gown billowed behind her slender figure, and her jewelry flashed like warning lights on top of a speeding ambulance.

"Mama!" Cordelia sat up hastily. "I'm glad you're feeling better."

"I got my medicine." Cordelia's mother lifted her crystal glass, which appeared to contain about one inch of clear liquid. "But I've only had one dose, dear, and it's not nearly enough—not this morning! Perhaps your, uh, friend would be so kind as to make me another?"

"Mama, it's not even lunchtime yet!"

"It's medicine, dear."

Geraldine fairly dropped the glass into Crash's hand, but he caught it deftly. "Sure thing, Mom. What'll it be?"

Although Princess Geraldine was nearly a foot shorter than Crash, she managed to look down her regal nose at him. "A martini, of course. It's the only truly medicinal drink in the world."

"I beg to disagree, Mom," Crash drawled. "I've been to a place where folks make a pretty mean corn liquor. That stuff can scale the insides off its own copper kettle."

"How charming," Geraldine said, all but lifting her lip with disdain. "Just make me a martini, dear. Can you do that? Cordelia keeps all her booze in the dining room. See how close you can come to making it correctly."

"Coming right up." Over Geraldine's head, Crash glanced at Cordelia merrily. "Anything for you— Sweetie Pie?"

"No, thanks, darling," Cordelia replied, giving him a steely look that ordered Crash to take it easy on the yahoo routine.

"Okeydokey. One martini."

As Crash sauntered out of the bedroom, Geraldine advanced on her daughter with an expression that meant business. "Cordelia," she said firmly, "I do not understand what you could be thinking. To throw away your whole future— It's incomprehensible to me."

Cordelia tried to gather her courage for the battle she knew was coming. "Then you haven't been listening, Mama. For years, I've been trying to tell you how I feel."

"But, darling!" Geraldine threw her arms wide to indicate the palace, the city, the country. "All this wonderful wealth, this power, this life! How can you turn your back on everything we've trained you for?"

"You haven't trained me for anything, Mama. Except how to throw money around. I'm not going to spend the rest of my life shopping!"

"We've carefully orchestrated your education—"

"Really?" Cordelia interrupted. "Mama, did you know I can ride a horse over Grand Prix jumps, but I can't write a check?"

"What's a check?" Geraldine asked blankly.

"Oh, Mama!"

"Well, it doesn't sound like a useful skill to me at all." The princess snorted and paced back and forth in front of the bed with her dressing gown floating out behind her. "Not compared to planning a state dinner or entertaining an ambassador. Why, you can write place cards better than any of your sisters, Cordelia! Why would you want to waste such a talent?"

"Because—"

"You're ungrateful!" Geraldine cried, throwing up her hands. "You don't know what it's like to be poor! Well, I've been poor, darling, and it's horrible! At my father's house, we barely had enough heat to keep warm in the winter!''

"Mama, that house was a castle in Norway, and you only stayed there in the summers. The rest of the time, you lived in sunny Italy."

"Well, it was unpleasant there, too. We couldn't afford proper servants. Why, even that awful automobile factory owner who lived next door to our villa kept a better chef than my family!''

"Believe it or not, I'd like to try living without a chef, Mama."

"You're insane! You've been brainwashed!"

"I have not."

"It's the end of the world for me! I'm going to faint! I'm going to die!''

"Hey!" Crash shouted.

Geraldine spun around to shriek at him, but he managed to wedge her drink into her hand just in time to shut her up. His quick move—not to mention his height and commanding tone—startled Geraldine into silence.

Gently, Crash said, "Yelling doesn't solve anything, and it upsets the baby."

Geraldine stared at him, then squinted nearsightedly to get a better look. Crash's innate virility must have impressed her, because Cordelia's mother did not speak for a long moment. Finally she said, "You're not so bad under those whiskers, are you?''

Crash grinned. "Why, thank you, ma'am. You're pretty nice to look at yourself."

Unnerved into blushing, Geraldine took three huge gulps from her drink to restore her composure.

"How is it?" Crash asked sweetly. "The drink, I mean?''

Her Royal Majesty gathered her wits and stared at her glass. "Heavens, you know how to make a martini!"

"It's an important life skill," Crash agreed.

"Do you really think so?"

"Sure," Crash said expansively. "It's mankind's most civilized drink—although not as good as corn liquor under certain circumstances. I learned the recipe from a bartender on Key West who said he used to make them for Ernest Hemingway."

Geraldine went on gazing at Crash with interest increasing every moment. "Ernest Hemingway," she repeated. "Did you hear that, Cordelia?"

"I heard, Mama."

"Do you know any other useful skills, young man?" Geraldine slurped more martini and leaned forward to listen attentively.

Crash's grin broadened as she warmed to him. "Well, ma'am, every man ought to know a couple of magic tricks and how to get the best table in a restaurant."

"Yes, yes, I quite agree."

"And how to find a cab on a rainy day at rush hour."

"Of course! What else?"

"Let's see. I guess he better know how to pick jewelry."

Geraldine's smile began to glow as brightly as sunshine. "Aren't you clever!"

"And, naturally, every man ought to know how to keep his little woman happy." To make his last point clear, Crash sat down on the bed behind Cordelia and put his arm around her possessively.

"'His little woman'?" Cordelia repeated, absurdly aware of the weight of his arm around her shoulders. The fingers of his right hand painted a tantalizing pattern on her arm.

As her anger deflated, Princess Geraldine sat down on the bed, too, not noticing that she slopped some of her martini on the pink satin spread. She had begun to look starry-eyed. "Do you love my daughter very much, Mr.—Mr.— Heavens, I don't even know your name!"

"Just call me Crash, ma'am. That's what this little filly calls me."

"Crash," Geraldine said meditatively. "Is that your given name?"

"Uh, no, ma'am. My mother called me Charles."

"Charles! Now, *that's* a nice name. A dignified name. Why, I have a second cousin by the name of Charles. He's the Prince of Wales. Do you know him?"

"Mama," Cordelia intervened severely, "Crash doesn't know any of the people we know."

"Oh, really? That's too bad." Disappointment clouded her face momentarily, but then Geraldine brightened once again. "We'll just have to introduce him around, won't we, dear?"

"Why?"

"To make him feel welcome, of course."

"Mama, the whole point is that Crash isn't one of us! He's a *commoner.*"

"Oh, I doubt he's common, dear. Why, look how attractive he is! Once we clean him up, I'm sure we'll find he's—"

"*Mama,*" Cordelia warned, "You're drinking too much medicine again."

"Just to dull the pain, dear."

Cordelia laughed. "You haven't known pain in your entire life."

Geraldine's mouth puckered into a pout. "Just wait until *you* have a daughter who runs away and gets married and has a baby without letting you even give a little *tiny* wedding! Now that's pain!"

"Mama, we're not married."

"You're not? Why, darling!" Geraldine's face lit up with boozy delight. "That means there's hope!"

"Hope for what?"

"A wedding, of course! A royal wedding!" Geraldine leapt to her feet and began to immediately plan the event, crowing, "It'll be more wonderful than my own! Oh, you don't know how long I've been dreaming of giving my girls their weddings! And yours must be the most grand, Cordelia. We'll have flowers by the trainload and caviar from my cousin the count and those lovely white horses your father raises—"

"I hate to spoil your dreams, Mama, but I have no intention of marrying."

Geraldine blinked and stopped fantasizing. "Whatever does she mean, Charles?"

"I'm afraid, ma'am," Crash said, sounding regretfully noble, "Slim means that I'm just not up to snuff. I'm the lousy son of a gun who got her preggers, and I know I've ruined her whole life, but . . . well—"

Geraldine leaned forward eagerly. "You do love her, don't you?"

Crash did a pretty fair imitation of an aw-shucks country boy embarrassed to reveal his emotions. He hung his head and drawled, "Well . . ."

"I knew it!" Geraldine cried, sloshing the remains of her drink on the carpet. "The moment I walked in,

I saw the electricity between the two of you! And you're not as bad as you think, Charles. You have a very aristocratic nose, for example. I bet if we looked back into your family tree, we just might find—"

"Don't you dare, Mama!"

"Why, darling, for all we know he *could* be perfectly acceptable husband material. All we have to do is—"

Cordelia leapt to her feet and snatched the empty glass from her mother's hand. "Don't go looking into any trees, don't do *anything*, do you hear? I'm ruined, soiled, spoiled, whatever you want to call it— and I just want to be left alone!"

"Slim—"

She whirled on Crash in a rage. "Don't call me Slim!"

"Darling, you're upset."

"You're damn right I am, Mama!"

"Slim, don't get yourself in a tizzy. Think of the baby."

"To hell with your baby!" Cordelia exploded, hurling the glass across the room. It shattered into a thousand pieces against the marble fireplace, but Cordelia never noticed. "Don't you see what she's trying to do? She wants you to be respectable!"

Princess Geraldine protested. "Oh, no, darling, it's *you* I want to be respectable! And if we find out that Charles is remotely connected to any royal family—"

"He's not!"

"Well, he *might* be. I know a wonderful genealogist—you know the one! He traced one hundred and twenty-two generations of William the Conqueror's illegitimate children. Now *that's* a challenge. If we put him on the trail—"

"Mama, I forbid you!"

"You can't forbid me, dear." Geraldine drew herself up to a noble—if slightly wobbly—posture. "I'm Her Royal Majesty, Princess Geraldine of Cordofino. Besides, Ida and Ada say they can't actually prove you've been to bed with this man."

Suddenly riveted to the floor with shock, Cordelia froze and stared. "They what?"

Crash asked, "Ida and Ada? Those two old biddies I met before?"

"They're Cordelia's Ladies of the Bedchamber." While Cordelia tried to regain her power of speech, Geraldine was happy to explain further. "Ida and Ada take care of my daughter's mundane household duties for the most part, and correspondence, staff organization, that sort of thing—"

"And they change the sheets," Crash said with a grin.

"It's barbaric, I know. But my husband's family is an ancient one. They believe they have been made royal by God, and you don't take that sort of responsibility lightly. If Ida and Ada say Cordelia hasn't been despoiled, then—"

"But I'm pregnant! Can't you see? How in the world do you think I got this way?"

Geraldine rose from the bed. "You never know, darling. Modern technology and all!"

"But *I* say—"

Geraldine patted Cordelia's hot cheek. "It doesn't matter what you say, darling. Remember your great-grandmother who wanted an annulment? When *her* Ladies of the Bedchamber couldn't produce the evidence of consummation, the pope was ready to grant her any wish she wanted. Oh, he was a dear man, the pope."

"As I recall, her husband locked her in the south tower for nine years until she gave in to him, so the annulment was off."

"Well, yes, so nobody gave a hoot what she had to say in the end. It was a man's world—and still is, in this family. I don't claim we're particularly sophisticated, darling, just old-fashioned in every noble sense of the word."

"Are you saying," Crash interrupted, "that even if Cordelia's blown up like a bitch with nineteen puppies, the official word is that she's still a virgin?"

"That's it, Charles." Geraldine waved jauntily and sailed for the door. "So I'm going to see a man about a genealogy chart, and Ida and Ada will keep an eye on the bedsheets, and you two—well, exercise some self-control for a few days!"

When Geraldine slammed out the door, Cordelia swayed on her feet and tried not to faint. Or scream with frustration.

"I like your mom," Crash said cheerfully. He relaxed back into the pillows and linked his hands behind his head. "She's got fire in her eyes."

"That's gin," Cordelia retorted, clenching her fists at her sides. "The old bat is due for her annual trip to the spa where she can dry out!"

"Take it easy, Slim," Crash said, eyeing her dubiously. "It won't do any good to get yourself worked up."

"I know what *will* do some good."

"What's that?"

"Take off your clothes," she ordered.

Five

Crash swallowed hard and watched her strip off the jacket of her suit, noting how her lovely round breasts strained against the wispy blouse she had worn under it. Any second, it looked like he might have his hands full of those breasts. In fact, he could have his *mouth* on her breasts and his hands up her skirt, if he chose, and within half an hour Crash Craddock could officially go down in history as the man who despoiled the princess of Cordofino.

"Wait a minute," he said, astonishing himself with a momentary burst of good conscience. "Hang on. Maybe you'd better think this through."

"I've already thought this through. The plan has changed. Unbutton me!"

She spun around, presenting the back of her blouse, lined with ten delicate pearl buttons. Obediently,

Crash began to unfasten them, but he said, "I don't know if this is in your best interest, Slim."

"I'm not paying you to think about my best interests, Crash. Just do it."

"Do it?" he repeated. "Do it, huh? How romantic."

"I don't need romance! I need blood on the sheets!"

"Well, that image sure gets me in the mood—not to mention a bedroom the size of Grand Central Station with a queen running in and out whenever she chooses and a bodyguard—where the hell *is* Rudi, by the way? How can I be sure he won't burst in and break my legs even if I do manage to work myself up to—"

"Don't worry," Cordelia snapped. "this won't take more than a few minutes."

"It's hardly worth doing if it only takes a few minutes."

As he finished unfastening her blouse, she turned around and ripped it off. She threw it on the floor and reached for the zipper on her skirt. It dropped to the floor, also, leaving Cordelia dressed only in a half-slip, lace panties and a pink flowered bra with a snap at the front. She reached for the snap, but there her hands hesitated.

She looked down at her belly, struck dumb by the size of her body. Then, softly, she said, "God, this is so gross."

"It's not gross." Crash said quite honestly, "I'll admit it's different for me, but it's sexy in its own way."

"I don't feel very sexy," she said in the same soft voice that trembled just a bit. Quickly she tried to control the tremble by tightening her jaw. "But that doesn't really matter, does it? If we get this over with and . . . and—"

"I don't think so, Slim." Gently, Crash continued, "I can't believe I'm saying this, but—"

"You don't have a say in the matter!" she cried, her eyes getting glassy with tears. "For a million dollars, you'll do what I want!"

"I'm not a million-dollar gigolo!" Crash's voice rose to match hers. "I said I'd come over here and tell everybody I was the father of your baby, but I never said I'd—"

"You think I *am* gross," she cried with all the logic of a near-hysterical woman. She backed away, tears threatening to spill any second.

"You're not gross."

"I *am!* You don't want to touch me!"

"I *do.* But I also don't want to land in the dungeon with your father waving hot pokers around my eyeballs!"

"You think I'm fat and disgusting!" she wailed.

"I do not! Slim—"

"You hate the sight of me!"

And then Cordelia burst into tears.

Hormones, Crash thought laconically. Female hormones caused all kinds of craziness, and a pregnant woman was bound to have moments of pure insanity.

Crash couldn't help reflecting that the subject of volatile female hormones was one of those facts of life a man just didn't learn in a junior high health class taught by a semiliterate football coach. They were a very important fact of life just the same, and any man who didn't recognize their power was doomed to a life of suffering at the hands of the occasionally berserk women around him.

Crash went over and took Cordelia in his arms. She collapsed against his chest and sobbed like a baby.

She smelled wonderful, though, and her bare skin felt delicious to Crash. Automatically he traced the line of her spine with his fingertips and said soothingly, "It's okay, Slim. You're not gross. You're beautiful no matter what shape you're in, and I—well, there's not a man on the planet who wouldn't scoot into that bed with you right now."

"Except you," she burbled against his shirt.

Crash sighed. "I just— It's not as simple as you think."

She cried harder. "Go . . . go ahead and say it. You . . . you can't bring yourself to look . . . look at me!"

"Looking's the easy part."

She jerked up her tear-stained face, eyes flashing with fury. "What does *that* mean?"

"Not what you think!" he said hastily, aware that his brain had momentarily short-circuited at the sight of the luscious fullness of her breasts threatening to spill over the top of her flimsy bra. Their cream-puff softness pressed delectably against his chest.

He stifled a groan. His own body had started to react instinctively to all her soft curves. Quickly he tried to back away. The last thing she needed was to feel a male erection throb against the lower curve of her belly. But she had an unbreakable grip on his shirt, and Crash had to hold still.

"Look," he said nervously, "why don't you sit down for a second, and I'll get you a glass of water."

"I don't want a glass of water."

"Sit down, anyway."

He forced her down on the bed, but she grabbed his hand to prevent his escape. "Wait." With a snuffle, she bowed her head. "Don't go."

"All right, all right. I'm staying." He stroked her hair. "Just keep your voice down. The whole palace can probably hear every word." He knelt down in front of her and steadied Cordelia with a hand on each of her hips, forcing her to look into his eyes. "Take a deep breath and think, okay?"

She blinked and huffed a breath. "O-okay."

Without being aware of his actions, he began to stroke Cordelia to calm her down. "Now, let's be logical for just a minute. Ready?"

A tear balanced itself on her nose. "R-ready."

Crash lifted one finger to wipe the tear away. "As I see it, your mama's grasping at straws. You've already got her beat, but she's trying to save the situation, right?"

"R-right."

He made his voice sound hypnotic, and he ran his fingers into her black hair to brush it rhythmically back from her face. "Your mom's just blowing hot air. The genealogist idea is a dead end, so her plan won't work. We both know that. And your dad's storming around the palace having fits, but he'll calm down soon, won't he?"

"Only if a guard shoots him with a tranquilizer dart."

For a moment Crash hoped the guards might actually carry such weapons, but he quickly banished the idea as the wishful thinking of a desperate man. "He'll exhaust himself eventually, Slim. See, all we have to do is ride this out. Before long, you'll be free, I'll have a million bucks and your sister will inherit the country. That's what you want, right?''

''Y-yes.''

''Everything's going according to plan. You just have to keep your head while the fireworks explode.''

''Crash—''

''It'll be okay,'' he said.

Suddenly he realized he'd progressed from stroking her hair to caressing her throat and bare, golden shoulder. Instead of hypnotizing her, he'd done it to himself.

As if from far away, she said, ''What are you doing, Crash?''

''Calming you down.''

''Oh.''

''Are you feeling calm?''

''I'm . . . feeling something, all right. But not . . . especially calm.''

Almost mechanically, Crash slipped her bra strap down her arm. He wasn't thinking, but his right hand instinctively skimmed downward from there to cup her breast. Although his brain began screaming for him to stop, Crash's thumb disobeyed and slowly circled the nipple. Mesmerized by the sight of his own hand touching her so intimately, Crash suddenly couldn't speak. Her nipple hardened into an erect peak beneath his thumb.

''Crash,'' she tried again.

''God, you feel good.''

Unsteadily she let out a sigh and didn't move as he made another slow exploration of her nipple with his thumb. She said, ''We . . . we still have something to prove to Ida and Ada.''

''Do we?''

"If my plan is going to work, yes."

"Which plan? You've got so many. God, you feel *really* good."

Maybe he was crazy. Maybe his own hormones were the cause of temporary insanity, but Crash flicked the catch on her bra, and it came miraculously unfastened. He caught his breath as it opened and his hand was filled with the most beautiful breast he'd ever touched. Pink and white, firm yet soft beneath his fingertips. Beautiful. Perfect.

She swiped her tongue across her lower lip as if suddenly parched, and she rested her hands on his shoulders. "I—I think we should still make love. It's logical."

"Logical?"

He went on caressing her breast with one hand, and used the other to slide her hips closer to the edge of the bed. Her skin whispered on the pink satin spread. Her knees parted, and Crash wedged himself between them, still kneeling.

Her voice trembled as she said, "Take a deep breath and think, Crash."

"I'm trying."

"When Mama discovers you're the lowliest commoner in the world, Ida and Ada still aren't going to believe we slept together. I never thought my family would fall back into the sixteenth century and demand that old bedsheet thing, but— *Oh.* Oh. That's nice."

He had wet his thumb with a lick, then circled her nipple over and over with liquid gentleness. He watched her shiver with pleasure.

"That's *so* nice," she whispered, closing her eyes.

Crash kept fondling her wet-smooth nipple and found himself simultaneously fascinated by the perfect, creamy flesh on the inside of her thigh. Yep, temporary insanity for sure. He lost his train of thought when he touched her there, too. "Er—we could try faking it. You know, by pricking your finger or something."

"Do you—o-oh—think that would work?"

"Hmm...I don't know."

"Don't you think—" She gasped as he reached the silky fabric of her panties with one finger. Her green eyes opened very wide. "Oh, my. Don't you think we should go through with the real thing?"

"Maybe."

"Just to be on the safe side."

Hoarsely he said, "Maybe it is the right move."

"Trust me. It's the only surefire way," she insisted.

"It's...logical, I guess."

She took another deep breath. "Do you mind? I mean, it was never part of our original agreement."

"Well, it's no problem." Crash found a tantalizing drop of dampness on the panties, and he circled it with a forefinger. "You're paying me a hell of a lot for everything else, the least I could do is..."

"You could...?"

"Sure. As a favor." Under his caress, the spot grew increasingly wet, a reaction that sent Crash's pulse soaring. He found a small button of hard flesh under the dampness and focused on that with a slow, circular motion.

Cordelia's hands tightened on his shoulders, and she gasped. "This is very—oh, my—nice of you, Crash."

"When do you suppose we should, uh, go through with it?"

"Oh—" She arched her back and shuddered. "Anytime."

"Like now, maybe?"

"Oh, Crash—"

"Now's a good time for me."

"How...how do we start?"

"I could pull your panties off like this."

"Oh, yes."

Tugging the lacy panties down to her knees required Crash to move out from between her thighs. As he stood, Cordelia put a tentative hand on his jeans. She looked up with her eyes turning smoldery and asked, "Does this help, too?"

"Yeah," he said with a convulsive gasp. Her palm made contact with the aching ridge beneath his zipper. "Yeah, that helps a lot. Now if you could..."

"This?" She unzipped his jeans.

"Good, good." Crash stripped off her panties and half-slip in one yank, then pushed her gently onto her back on the bed. "Yeah, this is very good."

"What next? I've never—"

"—done this before, I know. You're doing fine."

"Should we kiss?"

"Kissing's good. Absolutely."

He took her mouth then, in a wet, hot kiss that threatened to set them both on fire. Her lips tasted warm and inviting, and she made a little noise—half sigh, half moan. She wound her slim arms around his neck and half turned on her side to face him. Crash groaned in his throat and eased down onto the bed with her. He skimmed his hands down her smooth beach ball belly and found that her bare bottom fit perfectly into his palms.

All the while, their kiss grew more intense. She parted her lips, and Crash tasted her tongue with his. They played an erotic game, both breathing raggedly.

The insides of her thighs quivered as he coursed one hand up and down Cordelia's creamy skin. With each caress, Crash drew closer and closer to the spot that beckoned for his attention. She arched to meet his feather-light strokes until at last he closed his hand around her.

"Oh, Crash." She shivered with pleasure.

She was wet and hot, and he stroked her there. She fumbled with his jeans, and then he was in her hands, too.

"Not too fast," he coached. "Man, this is too fast."

"Am I doing something wrong?"

"No, no." But when she caressed him with a wonderfully soft touch, he gasped, "Yes! Oh, yes!"

"But Crash—"

"Don't stop. That's good." Aware that he was on the verge of babbling, Crash said, "That's— Oh, yeah."

He kissed her throat, nuzzled her collarbone and found her breast with his lips. His tongue rolled the nipple, and a delicious sweetness warmed his taste buds. Cordelia gave a quivery sigh.

She was so responsive. All those hormones had combined into a Molotov cocktail that only needed a small spark to start the explosion. Glad to see her so alive, Crash reveled in giving her even more pleasure.

Sucking gently on her breast, Crash eased one finger inside her. She was snug and melting to his touch. Perfect. Perfectly ready, perfectly eager. There was no cry of pain, no tensing with anxiety. She even rose to meet him as he moved slowly within her. Crash was delighted to hear her breathing change tempo to match his rhythm.

"Oh, Crash! Crash—" She arched against him, offering more.

Moments later he withdrew, ready to replace his gentle presence inside her with a much more powerful one. He reared up on one knee over her and prepared to yank off his jeans completely.

But a not-too-distant shout halted him.

"Hel-looo!" called a voice. "Cordelia, are you here?"

Cordelia's green eyes opened wide and fastened on Crash's with horror. "My sister!"

"Damn!"

Thinking fast, Crash grabbed up the pink satin bedspread and wrapped it around her quaking body. In another instant he fastened his jeans and sprang off the bed. He grabbed her up and sent Cordelia flying toward the bathroom. She fled, her black hair flying, her bare feet making no noise on the thick carpet.

Then Crash whirled around to face their intruder.

She was drop-dead beautiful.

She stopped in the doorway of the bedroom and stared at Crash with arched eyebrows and a cool smile dawning on her thin mouth. The white poodle in her arms snarled softly.

"Wow," the woman said, managing to sound husky and sexy at the same time. "Nobody told me you were gorgeous."

"Hi," said Crash, frantically trying to remember if he'd gotten his jeans zipped in time. He let his hand fall casually to check.

"Hi, yourself," she replied watching his hand with amusement. "I'm Angelique. Cordelia's younger sister."

She emphasized younger with a flirtatious smile.

Crash put out his hand to shake, then decided against it. Besides, the dog looked like the biting kind. Crash managed a grin instead. "Nice to meet you. I'm Crash."

"Crash, is it? What an unusual name. Do you crash parties?"

"Ha, ha." Feeling like a fool, Crash raked his hair off his forehead. "You must be looking for Cordelia."

Angelique strolled into the bedroom with her dog tucked in the curve of her arm. "Yes, I can't wait to see her. I hear she's as fat as a cow."

Angelique sat down on one of the wing chairs by the window, and she crossed her legs gracefully. The delicate folds of a frothy pink peignoir opened casually. She had good legs, too, although Crash couldn't help but note they weren't as nicely shaped as her sister's. Angelique had the same dark hair as Cordelia, but she wore it short and cut in spikes around her face like some kind of female vampire. Her features were classically beautiful, but cold. She studied Crash with an air of predatory bemusement.

"Oh, she's not fat." Truthfully, Crash said, "In fact, I've never seen her looking so good."

"Really?" Angelique pulled a package of cigarettes from her pocket. Next came a gold lighter, which she proceeded to hand to Crash with the obvious plan that he should light her cigarette. He did, and the dog growled as Angelique blew smoke. "How long have you known my sister, Crash?"

The truth was a little more difficult to word this time. "Oh," he said vaguely, "our paths crossed earlier this year."

"Not very long, then."

"Long enough." He grinned.

"So I hear." Angelique laughed and blew more smoke. The dog hunched in her lap, battening down his ears. The princess said, "Unfortunately, Mama and Papa aren't as delighted to make your acquaintance as I am."

"Well, that's the story of my life, I guess."

"I doubt that, Crash." Her gaze flickered up and down his body, briefly resting—or maybe it was just Crash's imagination—on the zipper of his jeans. She smiled slowly. "But our family tends to be overprotective when it comes to having men around. You understand, I'm sure."

"I'm starting to."

Angelique blew more smoke and laughed. "Be glad you're not the downhill ski champion I once brought to my apartment. Papa ordered our national guard through my bedroom window in the knick of time. They used bayonets. The poor fellow hasn't been the same since, but he *has* shaved a few seconds off his best time."

"And he has the national guard to thank for that."

"Or me," said Angelique, gloating.

At that moment Cordelia made her entrance from the bathroom. She had left the satin bedspread behind and was prettily attired in a pale green, silk bathrobe that floated around her body with diaphanous grace and flattered her golden coloring. Looking completely composed, she tended her long hair with a gold-handled brush.

She managed to appear surprised to see her sister in the room. "Angelique, how nice to see you!"

"And you, Cordelia."

Crash observed Angelique as she watched with slyly hooded eyes when Cordelia crossed the room and bent over the chair to kiss her cheek.

Cordelia said, "You're looking well, dear."

"And you," Angelique replied, "are looking better than I expected. My goodness, Cordelia, pregnancy agrees with you!"

"That's what I keep telling her," Crash said jovially.

Cordelia gave him a quelling look.

"But you *are* enormous," said Angelique, eyeing her sister's figure. "You'll have to start working with my personal trainer the *instant* your baby is born."

"Oh, she's in fantastic shape," Crash put in. "She'll probably want to get pregnant all over again, won't you, Slim?"

"Crash," Cordelia said from between clenched teeth, "why don't you freshen up for lunch?"

"Oh, I'm comfortable the way I am."

"Run along, dear," Cordelia said, steel in her eyes.

"Yes," Angelique said languidly. "We want to talk about you, Crash, so get lost for a while, won't you?"

Crash had a bad feeling in his gut, but he decided to do as he was told. He sketched a gracious bow and made an exit.

When he was gone, Cordelia looked at her sister and said bluntly, "Okay, Angel. Tell me what's going on. Everything, please."

Angelique sat forward in her chair with a conspiratorial smirk. "Mama sent me, but of course you guessed that."

"Of course. What does she want?"

"She's organizing the whole staff, Cordelia. She wants us all to keep you and that wonderful hunk of a man from going to bed together."

"What!"

"I know, it sounds crazy. I told her it was like closing the barn door after the horse was gone, but you know Mama. She didn't understand what I meant."

With a distracted frown, Cordelia asked, "Has she been drinking a lot lately?"

"Not too much." Angelique yawned and relaxed again. "Your arrival did send her straight to the liquor cabinet, but now she's got this plan about you and Crash. That should keep her too busy to get loaded."

"She thinks she can actually keep me from being with Crash, does she?"

Angelique laughed. "Oh, come on, Cordelia! You don't really want to subject yourself to that man, do you? More than you already have, I mean."

Cordelia glowered at her self-satisfied younger sister. "What have *you* got against him?"

"Well, he's terribly attractive, of course, but—really, dear. He's so *common*."

"Since when have you cared about the background of your various male friends?"

"They're my *friends*, Cordelia, not my lovers. Do you think I would jeopardize my chances of being a queen someday? That is, if something tragic ever happened to you, of course."

Wryly, Cordelia said, "It's nice to know you're so concerned about my well-being, Angel. You've sacrificed your love life for the chance to take over when Papa is gone?"

"I can have my fun in other ways," Angelique said with a wave of her beautifully manicured hand that indicated the whole wide world and all its possibilities. "But you—look at you! Do you honestly think you've made the right choice, dear?"

"Absolutely."

"And you're committed to this handsome commoner you've brought home to meet the family?"

"I'm committed to getting a new life," Cordelia said firmly.

Angelique raised her eyebrows. "You're avoiding my question. What about Crash?"

"What about him?"

"Is he worth giving up a throne for?"

Cordelia turned away nervously. "That's none of your business."

In an instant Angelique was on her feet and hanging over her sister's shoulder. "What's going on, Cordelia?"

"I thought it was obvious. I'm going to have a baby, and I'm leaving the family."

"For Crash?"

"Crash and I are—well, we haven't established what the future is going to be."

"But you do care for him?"

The question stumped Cordelia. If she'd been asked a few hours ago, she'd have honestly claimed she wouldn't care if Crash Craddock went off to join the Foreign Legion. But now—suddenly things felt different. Somehow Crash had managed to stir a lot of sexual thoughts that kept Cordelia from thinking clearly.

"Well?" Angelique prodded.

Cordelia spun around to face her curious sister. "Of course I care about Crash. He's the father of my child, isn't he?"

"And that's all?"

"Just— Oh, stop asking me such silly questions, Angelique." Cordelia managed a carefree laugh. "Surely you have something more important on your mind. Like, what you're going to do with Cordofino when Papa and I are out of the picture? Care to tell me all about your plans?"

With a smile, Angelique sat down again and began to regale her sister with royal fantasies. Angelique failed to notice when Cordelia's attention wandered back to thoughts of Crash and how it had felt to be in his arms.

Six

Shanghaied.

Crash figured he'd been royally double-crossed and shanghaied as soon as he found himself locked in a cold, stone room with no windows.

"Hey," he called through the door. "Rudi, old buddy, I think we made a wrong turn!"

He pounded on the heavy wooden door with his fist. No response. Rudi, it seemed, had taken a powder.

So much for lunch, Crash thought glumly, turning around to examine his cell. He'd gone looking for a sandwich and ended up imprisoned by a sneaky bodyguard.

The only light in the room came from the uneven crack under the door, but that was enough to see the rough shapes around him. Squinting, Crash could make out a spindly table, one wooden chair and a blanketless bunk. Classic dungeon decor.

Luckily, the former resident had left the lopsided remains of a candle on the table. Crash remembered pocketing Angelique's gold lighter, and he pulled it out. A moment later the room flickered with candle-light.

Beside the candle lay a leather-bound book, also left behind. Crash picked it up.

"The Man in the Iron Mask." He read the gold lettering on the spine of the volume out loud. "Very funny. I'm glad everybody has a sense of humor around here."

He dropped the book back onto the table and glanced around the dungeon again.

"Well, it's not bad," he muttered. "I've been in worse places."

He sat down on the chair to think things through.

In minutes he came to one conclusion about his situation. Well, two conclusions.

The first was that all he really wanted was the million dollars. The money was going to solve all his problems, make life easier, clean up a few outstanding debts and be a good start on the future. Every man should be so lucky. Who wouldn't want some extra cash to improve his situation? And for a million dollars, Crash was willing to spend a little time in a Cordofino dungeon.

The second conclusion was that Crash wanted the million dollars *and* he wanted to go to bed with Cordelia.

Simple as that. She was sexy as hell, and she obviously found him appealing, too. Mutual attraction was hard to fight. And they *did* have a baby between them, after all. It seemed like the stars were all in the right place. They were *meant* to fool around, he reasoned. Just once.

Well, maybe a couple of times, Crash thought a moment later. After all, there were a few lovemaking techniques he wanted to enjoy with her. His mouth got dry just thinking about the ways they could give each other pleasure.

He wasn't getting any closer to that goal by sitting here rotting in a cell, though.

But Crash thought about lovemaking, anyway, and let his imagination roam freely over the erotic possibilities. Eyes closed, Crash smiled at the fantasy of Cordelia's passionate sighs in his ears, her hot kisses on his mouth and her deliciously full body against his.

"But what if this jail term is her idea?" Crash said suddenly. "I wouldn't put it past the witch to lock me up if it suited her purposes."

And Rudi *was* Cordelia's servant, wasn't he? So who else would have given the order to imprison Crash for a while?

Not much time had gone by when his increasingly irritated thoughts were interrupted by a noise on the other side of the door, and soon a tray of food came sliding along the stone floor.

Crash jumped to his feet. "Hey!" he bellowed through the locked door. "I'm an American citizen, you know! The whole United States Marine Corps could parachute in here and rescue me any minute! Save yourselves the trouble and let me go right now!"

His jailer seemed unimpressed and walked away without speaking.

"Hey!" Crash shouted. "Rudi! Is that you? Can anybody hear me?"

Apparently not.

"I refuse to eat!" Crash bellowed after his retreated jailer. "I'm going on a hunger strike!"

He picked up the tray and discovered that prison food was a hell of a lot better than the burgers in Atlantic City greasy spoons. Waldorf salad, crab patties, asparagus, three tiny red potatoes, and a fluted glass filled with chocolate raspberry mousse were all arranged on the wicker tray decorated with red-and-white checked picnic napkins and a small vase sporting an assortment of wildflowers. The beverage choices included a liter of bottled water, a carafe of white wine and a silver pot filled with hot coffee.

"No sense starting a hunger strike yet," he muttered to himself. "After all, I have to keep my strength up."

Crash sat down and ate his lunch with gusto.

"My compliments to the chef," he said when he'd finished the mousse.

After lunch, he carried a cup of coffee and *The Man in the Iron Mask* over to the bunk. He made himself comfortable and proceeded to spend the afternoon rereading a book he had enjoyed years ago. Reading felt a hell of a lot more productive than fuming about Cordelia.

When jet lag and the rich meal joined forces to put Crash to sleep, he dozed for a while with the book open on his chest. He wasn't sure how long he'd slept when a noise outside the door woke him to darkness. The candle must have guttered out at last. The sound of a key turning in the lock was unmistakable, and Crash sat up groggily on one elbow.

When the door swung wide, it was Cordelia herself who stepped into the dark room. From the corridor behind her streamed daylight, silhouetting her figure for Crash's pleasure.

"You and your sister must have the world's largest collection of erotic lingerie," he said thickly.

"This is not erotic," she retorted, advancing on him.

"Oh, no? I can see right through it."

"You can not!"

"Can, too. Your panties are blue."

She gave a yelp and darted sideways out of the light. "Must you be such a lout?" she said with exasperation.

"Sorry, Slim, but a leopard can't change his spots— even in jail. I have no class, and I probably never will." Crash sat up and swung his legs over the edge of the bunk.

He decided her outfit wasn't erotic, after all. Cordelia had slipped into another long, flowing robe with a high, lace collar and prim schoolmarm sleeves. The white silky fabric *was* see-through, but only when the light was behind her, he saw with disappointment. Her slippers were low-heeled and trimmed with some kind of white feathers. Her pregnancy was still prominently displayed but so were her long legs, graceful neck and lovely bosom. A froth of lace outlined their shape. Her dark hair tumbled around her shoulders in disarray, as though she'd been scouring the palace for hours.

"I'll always be a lout. But you look good, though."

"No thanks to you," she said tartly. She grabbed the book from him, noted the title and threw it back onto the bunk. Then she glared at Crash with her fists cocked on her hips, eyes blazing. "Where have you been?"

"Where the hell does it look like I've been? Here in jail, thanks to you."

"Thanks to me? I had nothing to do with this!"

"Oh, no?"

"I've been looking for you for hours! I thought you decided to run away or maybe my mother—" But she caught herself and made a visible effort to calm down. "Well, I shouldn't have worried, I guess. You're here and you're reasonably healthy."

"Reasonably. But I hope you're going to have Rudi drawn and quartered."

"Rudi! Rudi did this?" A stormy look crossed Cordelia's face. "I guess it's time to remind Rudi exactly who pays his salary every month."

"Why don't you just fire him?"

"Because I need him," Cordelia said sharply.

It didn't take a genius to read her unspoken message. *Crash, old buddy, you're a temporary fixture in this lady's life, whereas Rudi is undoubtedly going to stick around for years to come. Don't expect her to trust you.*

"The bad news," Cordelia said abruptly, "is that my entire family has united to keep us apart. So we must be more careful. No more wandering off, do you understand?"

"I was hungry! I went looking for a sandwich."

"I'll show you how to ring for service," she said sternly. "In the meantime, follow me back to my apartment. And don't go wandering off by yourself anymore."

"Maybe we ought to stay here for a while. If you're worried about my safety, that is. And it's certainly private."

If she guessed his meaning behind the suggestion, Cordelia chose to ignore the implication. "It's time to dress for dinner."

With a sigh, Crash eased off the bunk. "I think I like you better *un*dressed, Slim."

She cast a wry glance over her shoulder. "Not with my father in the room, I'm sure."

"Why does he have to be with us?"

"He's finally stopped lugging his sword around threatening to make sure you'll never father any more bastards, as he so delicately puts it. We've been summoned to a family dinner."

Crash caught her arm and pulled Cordelia around to face him. "I thought we could have a quiet little supper together. Just you and me."

She didn't pull away but refused to look up at Crash. "We can't. Not tonight, at least."

"I thought you wanted—"

"I know, I know."

"Nervous?" Crash asked, suddenly putting two and two together.

She did raise her head and looked at him then with those fantastic green eyes. "I'm not the nervous type."

But she was lying, Crash knew at once. Beneath his grasp, he could feel a slight tremble in her arm.

All she needs is a little convincing. She was in the mood before. Trouble is, she's had time to get embarrassed. And scared.

"What's the matter?" he asked, gently massaging the tension from her arms.

"Nothing. I—I've been thinking, that's all."

"About what?"

"About the future. My future. It's complicated enough without—well, you and I—I just think it's best to keep things simple."

Crash took his hand from her arm. "You've changed your mind about going to bed?"

"No, no." Her cheeks turned pink and she shook her head rapidly. "But I don't want to get involved. I want us—this whole thing to remain a simple business deal."

"Sex can be simple."

"Yes, but—"

"What's got you so upset?" With a laugh, he asked, "Afraid we're going to fall in love or something? You—the princess? Me—the bum?"

"Stranger things have happened," she said tartly, quickly turning away from Crash. "Come on. We're going to be late for dinner."

Crash didn't follow her at once. He hesitated, frowning. He had the uneasy feeling that things had started to get even more complicated.

Thank heaven for good manners, Cordelia thought at dinner that evening.

A member of the royal family would rather die than squabble in front of the household servants, so nobody said a word out of order during the five-course meal that took place in the family dining room on the third floor.

Prince Henri sat silent and stone-faced at the head of the table, occasionally glowering at Cordelia, who sat a comfortable fifteen feet away from him. His temper did not affect his appetite, she noticed, for he appeared to eat every crumb on his plate and even devoured a heap of chocolate-dipped strawberries for dessert.

Cordelia's youngest sister, Julianna—looking more muscular than ever—picked at her dinner and seemed to examine every morsel for fat grams before she put a forkful into her mouth. She disapprovingly observed her father's intake and once ventured to say, "Papa, did you know there's absolutely no food value in salad dressing? You should eat your greens plain— or with a squirt of lemon at the very most."

Papa didn't answer, but slathered more butter on a roll and wolfed it down without appearing to chew.

The meal might have passed in complete silence except for Angelique and Princess Geraldine, who applied all their combined social skills on Crash.

Cordelia watched, frowning, as they gushed over him from both sides.

"Tell us about your family, Charles," Geraldine urged on several occasions.

"Yes, do tell us," Angelique agreed, propping her elbow on the table and leaning toward Crash as if fascinated. Her dog Muffin, perched on the chair next to hers, alert for handouts. "I'm sure your life is an amusing story."

"It's pretty ordinary, actually," Crash responded pleasantly.

He looked amazingly handsome in a borrowed dinner jacket, with his hair slicked back Humphrey Bogart-style and his face freshly shaven. In fact, Cordelia was astonished to see how well he cleaned up. If he didn't open his mouth, he might be mistaken for a prince himself.

But he said, "Actually, my mama was never completely sure who my pop was. For most of her life she was a showgirl, see, in New York. After I came along, she hit the road, and I went to live with some old friends of hers in Galveston, Texas. But she kept hoofin' all her life.''

"How delightful," Geraldine said, clapping her hands. "In show business! Did you hear that, Henri?"

Prince Henri didn't answer. Looking thunderous, he speared more strawberries from the crystal bowl offered by one of the footmen.

Angelique said, "And where did your mother come from originally, Crash?"

"Oh, from Paris, she always claimed. But I think it was more like Brooklyn. She had a great imagination!"

"She's no longer with us?" Geraldine inquired, leaning forward to refill Crash's wineglass.

Crash thanked her and drank more wine before saying, "No, Mama died about ten years ago—during a road production of *Kiss Me Kate.*" He hesitated, then added in a voice slightly softer, "I was in the merchant marines at the time, so I didn't find out about her death for a couple of months."

"How tragic! How did she die?"

"Heart attack on stage. Oh, she'd have wanted it that way, I'm sure. She always loved to tap dance." Enjoying being the life of the party, Crash regained his hale humor and swigged more wine. "By the time I got home, they'd already buried her in Boston. Boy, did I have to go through a lot of red tape finding the right cemetery!"

"I hope they got her name right on the headstone."

"Oh, sure!" he answered promptly. "Madeline Marie Craddock, just the way she spelled it in all the programs."

Cordelia knew exactly what her mother was up to and decided to intervene before Geraldine pumped every smidgen of information out of Crash. "Why don't you tell everyone about your boat, Crash?"

"'Boat'?" Geraldine repeated, blinking at Cordelia with puzzlement. "What does that have to do with anything?"

Angelique leaned even closer to Crash. "Oh, I'd love to hear about your boat, Crash. Do you like yacht racing?"

"Hell, no, you can't catch any fish going above ten knots." Expansively, Crash said, "I do deep-sea fishing, see, and the best way to catch the big ones..."

Cordelia seethed inside. Any minute, she expected Angelique to throw herself straight into Crash's plate and offer herself like some kind of exotic sacrificial virgin. And Geraldine was practically taking notes about Crash's family. It was damned annoying.

At the same time Cordelia could hardly forget what was in store for her later. With pins and needles in her veins, she remembered the afternoon scene in her bedroom. They had come so close! She could almost feel the gentle caress of Crash's hands. If she closed her eyes, she could imagine how aroused she might become if he touched her the same way again. And tonight...

Cordelia flushed and fidgeted in her chair, remembering her conversation with Angelique. Had her feelings about Crash changed? Was it possible to keep their relationship purely businesslike?

Watching Crash laugh at something clever Geraldine had said, Cordelia felt a ridiculous rush of jealousy.

Why should I care if he likes my mother? she asked herself. *Why does it make me angry to see him leer down the front of Angelique's dress? It's a stupid dress, anyway. Doesn't she see how foolish she looks in it—practically flaunting her bare breasts under his nose?*

Just take him to bed tonight, Cordelia commanded herself. *Then everything will be fine. You can send him back to the States tomorrow, if you like.*

Cordelia glowered at Crash as he went on burbling happily—clearly enjoying the spotlight that Cordelia's mother and sister directed at him. For two hours that evening, Crash entertained with all his stories of fishing, carousing and otherwise misbehaving himself. With growing exasperation, Cordelia noticed that her mother and sister seemed fascinated by everything Crash said. They frequently applauded and cheered his exploits.

The whole time, Cordelia thought alternately about murdering the man—and making wild love to him until he collapsed from exhaustion. He talked and laughed while Cordelia wished he'd just shut up and take her to bed.

But without warning, Crash suddenly gave a huge yawn. "Wow," he said, looking dazed. "I guess the jet lag is finally catching up to me."

"Tired, Crash?" Angelique asked, concernedly placing her hand on his arm.

"Yeah." He yawned again. "Suddenly I can hardly keep my eyes open."

"I think it's time we all retired," Geraldine said then, standing and addressing her husband. "You don't mind skipping the cigar ritual, do you, Henri?"

Julianna said, "Cigars are even worse than cigarettes, you know."

Without a word, Prince Henri harrumphed and got up from the table. He threw down his napkin and stalked from the room without a word.

Crash got to his feet, too, but he swayed dangerously and had to catch his balance on the table.

"A little too much to drink, Charles, dear?" Geraldine inquired.

"I guess so," he mumbled, clutching his forehead. "That's pretty potent wine you have in this country."

Cordelia stood in agitation. "Crash—"

Geraldine intervened. "The wine *is* delicious, isn't it? Angelique, why don't you step outside and ask Rudi to help Charles up to bed?"

"Of course, Mama."

Cordelia watched the whole farce with rage boiling inside herself. "You did this on purpose, Mama!"

Geraldine slipped an arm around Crash to prevent him from keeling over onto the table. "Did what on purpose, dear?"

"You drugged him!"

"Wha—" Crash made a valiant effort to control himself, but he suddenly staggered backward and fell into his chair once more.

Cordelia rushed to his side and peeled back Crash's limp eyelids. His pupils were enormous. "You *did* drug him! Mama, you've sunk lower than I ever imagined! How could you do something like this?"

"I haven't any idea what you're talking about," Geraldine said airily. "Oh, there you are, Rudi! Mr.

Craddock has had a teensy bit too much to drink. Will you be so kind..."

Rudi answered by hoisting Crash's limp body over his shoulder in a fireman's carry. Crash gave a goofy laugh and then fell completely unconscious.

Cordelia smothered a scream of frustration.

Angelique put her arm around Cordelia. "What's the matter, sis? It's just one night, you know."

But an important night, Cordelia knew. If her whole family had begun to conspire against her, she knew she'd have to be extra wily to outwit them. Through clenched teeth, she said, "I can't believe you'd do this to me."

"It's in your best interests, Cordelia, believe me."

"But if I leave the family, *you'd* be next in line!"

Angelique laughed and walked away. "Are you kidding? You really think I'd *want* the job? Don't be ridiculous!"

"But I'm unhappy!" Cordelia cried. "Doesn't anybody care?"

"You think you'd be happier with that man? Heavens, Cordelia, he's not one of us. Surely you see that."

Left alone in the dining room, Cordelia realized that her own family didn't give a damn whether she was happy or not. Oddly enough, a man she hardly knew cared more than her own flesh and blood.

Cordelia hastened out the door and up the stairs, following Rudi and an unconscious Crash to her apartment.

Twenty years later, Crash woke up. At least, it felt like twenty years. His brain felt two sizes larger than his skull, and a taste something like unleaded gasoline lingered in his mouth. He tried not to move. Every muscle was on fire. Every bone felt as if it had been systematically broken by a Sumo wrestler.

He opened one eye and was nearly blinded by the blazing light overhead. His voice broke as he croaked, "Somebody shoot me!"

He hurt everywhere. His head, all his joints. Even his *hair* hurt.

"Let me die," he begged his tormentor.

But when he opened both eyes, he was alone.

The room spun around his prostrate body like a kaleidoscope on Benzedrine. Pain racked every nerve-ending. His stomach gave ominous heaves. Crash groaned.

Then a face loomed over his. Cordelia said, "Awake, finally?"

"Wha-what—"

"You were drugged."

It was safer not to speak, so Crash just raised his eyebrows inquiringly.

"My mother," Cordelia explained, smoothing a blessedly cool cloth across his thundering forehead. "At least, that's who I'm putting my money on. She wanted to be sure we'd keep our hands off each other last night, so she slipped a mickey into your drink."

"Bu-but—"

"It's all right. You're going to live. I called a doctor to check on you this morning when you didn't wake up."

"'Time izzit?"

"Late afternoon. You slept like the dead."

Groaning again, Crash tried to roll over onto his side. It was agonizing, but he made it. There, he clutched the edge of the bed and hung on for dear life while it spun around. In a moment everything stopped spinning and settled into a relatively painless rocking.

Cordelia sat down beside him and placed one hand on his forehead. "You're looking better, I must say."

"I am?"

"Much better, believe me." Her hand slid down to his chest and stayed there, warm and soothing. "The doctor said you ought to eat something."

"Not unless you want to see me throw up."

"Hmm," she said, considering the situation. "I guess this means sex is out of the question?"

"I never thought I'd hear myself say this," Crash moaned, "but sex is the *last* thing on my mind right now."

She sighed. "Okay. I've got some work to do. Why don't you sleep a little longer and we'll try the toast later?"

"Yeah, later. Like a week or two."

Those were the last words Crash remembered saying. He felt Cordelia's hand lingering on his chest and enjoyed the sensation. Nice to have a woman around. Then darkness swirled up around him again.

The last thing Crash realized before he slept was that he was naked.

Seven

While Crash slept, Cordelia spent a busy two days getting back into the swing of palace life. Her unprecedented eight-month absence called for a tremendous amount of catch-up.

She met with her staff to plan menus, organize her wardrobe and schedule her appointments and activities. Giving special orders to Ada, she saw that Crash's clothes were laundered and others were purchased for him. There were also a hundred small issues that had arisen during her time away from home, so Cordelia dealt with everything from internal squabbles to writing sizable checks to charities and political organizations who had asked for her help. She made phone calls to her financial manager in Cordofino, her decorator in Milan and her personal shopper in Paris.

Later, she used her computer to compose a letter to the U.N. on behalf of Muslim refugees. Then she faxed a message to the March of Dimes, agreeing to help with next year's campaign. And finally, she wrote a private note to her cousin, a Spanish prince, congratulating him on winning a fencing tournament in Rome and— "By the way, Juan, dear"—asking for his support in negotiating a problem between a Spanish and a Cordofinian bank.

She was interrupted at teatime by the unexpected arrival of her father.

His Royal Highness was accompanied by a frightened footman carrying a tea tray that rattled as he trembled. At the appearance of the prince's scowling face, Cordelia's staff—Ida and Ada, plus the personal secretary, George—bolted for cover, all babbling their excuses and bowing hastily to the prince before escaping like a bunch of terrified rabbits.

Prince Henri chose the sofa near the French window and sat down in silence, waiting until the footman had poured their tea and departed.

Cordelia set her eyeglasses on the desk, then went to sit down on the brocade chair opposite her father. "Well, Papa? Have you come to glare at me, or do you plan to speak to me at last?"

Prince Henri picked up a teacup and waited until he heard the click of the door behind the footman before he broke his silence. Then, in his most cold and princely tones, Cordelia's father said, "I have come to discuss the mess you've gotten yourself into."

"It's not a mess from my standpoint, Papa."

"Then you're more foolish than I thought." The prince put his cup down abruptly, splashing tea on the low table. "I have always expected reckless behavior from your sisters, Cordelia, but never you."

"Then you misjudged my character."

"I don't think so," he said severely. "You're the intelligent one. Angelique is just like her mother—concerned with her own pleasures and nothing else. Your sister Julianna has become obsessed with her own body. She was always the narcissistic one, but I never thought it would go as far as weight-lifting contests! But you, Cordelia—you are the one I had high hopes for."

"I never asked for any of this, Papa."

Sitting very erect on the sofa, Prince Henri regarded her solemnly. He was every inch a royal prince at that moment—handsome, correct, stiff yet unerringly polite even when he was delivering a lecture. He held on to his temper, but just barely. His green eyes—the same vibrant green as Cordelia's own—blazed brightly with suppressed emotion.

Underneath his stoic frown boiled a rage that Cordelia had only glimpsed a few times in her life—once during a humanitarian visit to a Bosnian hospital and once during a celebrity tennis tournament with Don Rickles. In both cases, Prince Henri had unleashed a fury unmatched by any volcanic eruption.

Sternly he said, "None of us has asked for this life, Cordelia. But we must carry on."

"Carry on? That sounds like a pack animal loaded up with firewood!" Determined to make him understand, Cordelia leaned forward in her chair. "I can't spend my life carrying the load, Papa."

Henri got up quickly. "You sound like a spoiled little girl!"

"I never had a chance to be a little girl," she retorted. "Maybe it's time I tried it!"

"Don't be ridiculous!" The prince began to pace, looking elegant but angry at the same time.

"Everyone deserves some happiness, Papa. Even princesses."

"Were you ever unhappy?" he demanded. "You never lacked for anything!"

Except affection, Cordelia thought. But she could not wound her father with those words. Instead she said, "It's not *things* I wanted, Papa. I just want to be myself."

"You are a princess!"

"I am a woman! I want the same things other women want!"

"Like what?"

"Like love. A family. Children."

"We've made every effort to see you happily settled with a suitable husband."

"Too bad the selection has been so thin," she said sharply. "You and mama have paraded every nobleman left in the civilized world before me, and I thank you for all your efforts. But none of them are remotely what I want in a partner."

"We'll keep looking."

"The prince hasn't been born who will make me happy!"

Prince Henri sketched an impatient, dismissive gesture with one hand. "What is happiness, anyway? A state of mind created by empty-headed fools!"

"How can you say that?" Cordelia asked, amazed. Then she collected herself and said earnestly, "I want something important to do with my life. I'm intelligent and talented in many ways, and I want meaningful work. And I want to breathe, Papa, to be free and unchained—"

"Do you think I don't experience the same desires?" Henri halted before her, staring down at Cordelia with his hands clasped firmly behind his back and his face a mask of control. "I'm only human, too. Of course I wish I had no responsibilities, no cares! But I go play tennis or golf or ride my horses and the feeling goes away."

"Papa—"

The prince railroaded over her words. "I have been chosen by God, Cordelia, and by the noble people of this country. I do not take my destiny lightly. I have work to do, and I have done it! Do you think Cordofino was always so beautiful? So rich? Do you think our schools magically became among the best in the world? No! I can look upon these achievements and know that *I* created them."

"I know you've worked hard, Papa. But what is there left for me to do after you? This is the world's most perfect country—"

"You *are* a fool if you believe that!"

"What do you mean?"

"You are blind to our problems? Have you been so busy buying clothes from Paris that you have not seen the ugly side of Cordofino? Can't you see work in the world? We are blessed with power—power that can be used in many countries, not just our own." Bitterly he said, "I have been remiss, after all, haven't I? Perhaps you are as self-absorbed as Julianna, after all."

"I'm not!"

"Then as empty-headed as Angelique," he snapped angrily. "Life is what you make of it, Cordelia."

"I'm trying to make something of it."

"With that...that man you dragged in here?"

Cordelia nearly told him the truth, then. She had bought Crash's services only to gain her freedom. But if the prince knew what she'd done, the jig would be up. So Cordelia held her tongue on the subject of Crash and let her father think whatever he chose.

"You have accomplished nothing by taking this ruffian into your bed." The prince frowned uncomfortably out the window, and then he said in a different tone, "Unless you haven't actually done it."

"Done what, Papa?" Cordelia asked, suddenly feeling angry enough to torment him.

The prince pretended to be fascinated by the view from Cordelia's window. "Unless you haven't actually... fornicated with that commoner."

"I'm carrying his baby, aren't I?"

Prince Henri shot a skewering glare in her direction. "I'd like to be sure of that."

"Do you want me to submit to some kind of medical test? A doctor could tell you at once who the father is."

"I will accept your offer to take such a test," said the prince, narrowing his gaze on her. "I remember how well you bluffed at poker on our yacht cruises. But the Ladies of the Bedchamber also question the... conception of this child. Your mother believes..."

He hesitated and turned a livid shade of red.

"Yes?" Cordelia asked coolly.

Abruptly, Henri strode closer to the window and glared out at the sky. "Your mother has a wild imagination. She believes you might have accomplished this condition in some... unnatural way."

"What do you think?"

Henri turned back and raised a brow at Cordelia. "I have agreed to let her proceed in any way she chooses to end this situation."

"It won't do any good."

"Nevertheless, we will try anything."

Cordelia heard his resolution, and a wave of sadness crept into her soul.

"Papa, can't you just let me go?"

Prince Henri of Cordofino stiffened ramrod straight again. The blaze of battle gleamed in his green eyes. "I am sworn to protect my kingdom at any cost, young lady. The future of Cordofino is in my hands. And I must choose my successor to this noble calling. You, Cordelia, named after my beloved country on the day you were born, are my choice. I will do everything in my power to see you reign after I am dead."

"I don't want to!"

"Destiny cannot be changed."

"I'm not fit to sit on your throne! I've broken family law! I'm ruined—"

"Not yet," the prince corrected.

Seething, Cordelia cried, "Do you think you can pretend I'm not pregnant? A hundred photographers took my picture yesterday!"

"Your mother has circulated the story that you were playing a practical joke."

Cordelia leapt to her feet. "You can't cover this up, Papa!"

"Perhaps not. But we can certainly postpone the problem until we have devised a way to deal with it."

Unsteadily, Cordelia reached for the wing of a chair to steady her balance. Harshly she whispered, "What are you trying to do?"

"That," he said with a trace of smug superiority, "is a secret between your mother and myself."

"I demand to know!"

"You can demand until you are blue in the face. Rest assured that your mother and I are not taking this situation lying down. For the next several days you will remain in the palace—"

Cordelia cried, "I'm going straight out into the street to tell the whole world about this baby—"

"I forbid you to show yourself!" the prince commanded in a shout. "I will post palace guards outside your door, if I must!"

He would, too. Cordelia could plainly see his determination.

For the first time since setting out on her plan, Cordelia realized exactly what kind of force she was up against. She had never seen her father look so steadfast. He was as unyielding as Gibraltar.

She sank down on the sofa, not defeated, but suddenly very tired.

Sounding in control again, the prince said, "In a few days when the festival is over, the family will deal with your...indiscretion. Until then, please remain here and do nothing to make the situation worse."

Cordelia did not answer.

"Do you hear me?" he asked.

"Yes," she replied coldly.

Prince Henri took his leave without another word. The door clicked shut behind him.

When he was gone, Cordelia felt her baby stir. A lump rose in her throat, so she got up and paced restlessly. She ended up at her desk again and sat down on the chair. Again, the baby rolled in her belly as if reminding her there was no turning back.

Burying her face in her hands, Cordelia fought off the urge to cry.

From the doorway Crash said, "Well, at least he didn't have you beheaded."

Cordelia hastily pulled herself together.

Crash had wrapped a sheet loosely around his hips and looked like a slightly bleary centerfold as he lounged in the doorway and raked his hair back from his face.

"How much did you hear?" Cordelia asked.

"Most of it. He's serious, I think."

"Yes, I think he's very serious." Cordelia turned her back to Crash and pretended to rearrange the papers on her desk.

Crash sauntered over, holding the tied ends of the bedsheet closed with one hand. He leaned against the desk beside Cordelia and crossed one bare ankle over the other. She didn't look up, but he said, "Your father knows what he wants."

She nodded. "And he's plotting something to get it."

"What do you think he's going to do?"

"I don't know. I never thought beyond this point. I thought he'd give me up without a fight."

"Oh, he's ready to fight, all right."

"I know. It makes me..."

"Scared?"

"No," she said at once, fingering her eyeglasses idly. "Not scared. Sad."

Crash didn't answer for a moment. He glanced down at the desk and noticed the framed photograph of Cordelia's father in the clutter. It was a snapshot of Prince Henri, looking very young but gallant in his World War II uniform. He had been a pilot, flying relief supplies all over Europe. It was Cordelia's favorite photograph, but she said nothing as Crash ran a thoughtful finger down the frame.

Then he studied the collection of papers spread all over the desk. "What have you been doing here?"

"Tending shop," she said with a shrug.

"You mind?" He leaned over and reached for the two letters she had written before her father had arrived.

The last rays of sunlight streamed through the window over Cordelia's desk, throwing Crash's nearly naked physique into wonderful relief. The light seemed to glow on his hard chest and lithe arms. Cordelia almost set down her glasses and reached out to touch him as he skimmed the letters. She felt the unmistakable tug of attraction to his body.

But there was something even more likable about Crash, she thought to herself. Unlike her father, he was open and talkative. Yielding at times, but strong, too. He hadn't been afraid to say what he was thinking and feeling from the moment they'd met.

"Not bad," Crash said, still reading the letters. "You write well."

Bitterly she muttered, "I guess I learned something besides ballroom dancing at finishing school."

"Is this the kind of stuff you do all the time? Letters and business like this?"

"Yes," she said impatiently. "A lot of busywork, as you can see. Nothing important."

"It sounds important to me. This bank thing, for example." He held up the letter. "It's complicated. Do you understand the details?"

"It's not rocket science."

Crash glanced down at her speculatively. "You're belittling yourself. And the Muslim refugees. You're really passionate about helping them, aren't you?"

Relieved to put her own troubles aside at last, Cordelia said, "They're in a terrible situation. Women and children are hungry and homeless. Who wouldn't be passionate about their problems?''

''Not everybody's doing something about them, though.''

''I'm not doing much.''

Crash dropped the pages back onto her desk. ''Why are you so determined to run down your work here?''

''Let's not talk about work,'' Cordelia said abruptly. That terrible lump was back in her throat and she wanted to dispel it once and for all. ''I'd much rather hear about how you're feeling.''

He gave her a lazy grin. ''I'm okay, no thanks to your conniving mother. How long have I been sleeping?''

''Two nights and a day.''

''Wow.'' He raked his hair back and grinned sheepishly. ''I guess I deserved it. I acted like an ass at dinner.''

''That's what I pay you for,'' Cordelia said sharply, then instantly regretted her tone. ''Hungry?''

''A little.''

''There's tea on the table. Help yourself. And afterward...''

''Yes?''

In a rush Cordelia said, ''Let's go to bed.''

Crash laughed, dark eyes suddenly aglitter as he gazed at her. ''You didn't hear a word your father said, did you?''

''I heard every word! I'm choosing to ignore them all.'' She got up from the chair hurriedly and crossed the carpet to the tea tray. She poured Crash a cupful, splashing tea in all directions. From the serving plates, she selected two watercress sandwiches and a chocolate cookie. She balanced them on the saucer, despite the trembling in her hands. Quickly she said, "I knew from the beginning this part was going to be difficult. I just never imagined he'd react so badly. But I'll win. You'll see. Here."

Unceremoniously, she thrust the cup and saucer into Crash's free hand.

He wryly eyed the tea and food. "You think this is enough to keep my strength up?"

"I'll order you a steak dinner, if it will get you into bed quickly."

"Boy, you're a romantic lady, Slim." Crash grinned. "I'm not sure I can hang on to my passions much longer."

"We don't need romance or passion. This is a business deal, remember?"

Crash set the tea down on the desk, his grin fading. "I remember. I'm just not so sure you're on the right track anymore, that's all."

"I don't care what you think!" Cordelia retorted. "I just want your body for a few minutes."

"And I'm happy to give it," he shot back. "Except I can't help wondering if you're doing the right thing now."

"Of course I am!"

"Your old man thinks otherwise."

"I don't care what he thinks! I'm making decisions for myself." Cordelia grabbed the sheet that was tucked around Crash's hips. She tugged, "I want my freedom, Crash. And you're going to help me get it."

"What's so bad about living in a place like this?" Crash watched her face. He didn't resist as Cordelia tried to untie the bedsheet that clasped his hips. "You've got everything a human being could want."

"Not everything. This is a gilded cage, Crash."

"An awfully comfortable cage, though."

He held still as Cordelia finally managed to unfasten the sheet. Gently she slid one hand inside and found his naked hip. She stepped closer, running her caress around his behind—hard and smooth to the touch. Seductively, Cordelia said, "I'd like to make you comfortable for a little while, Crash."

"In bed, right?"

"Are you up to it? I mean, if you're still feeling sick—"

"I'm not sick. I'm having second thoughts, though."

She stopped caressing him and looked up with a frown. "What second thoughts?"

Crash wrapped one hand around her wrist. He shook his head. "Maybe Pop is right. If *my* father had said the things your father just said to you, maybe things would be different for me right now."

"Your father?" Cordelia cocked her head. "I thought you never knew your father."

"Well, of course," he agreed quickly. "I mean, if I *had* known him and if he'd said those things to me, I might have—well, the point is maybe you belong here, Slim."

"Crash," she said sweetly, clenching her teeth to keep from screaming. She edged sideways so her belly wasn't an obstruction between them and pressed close. "Crash, let me decide about my own future. You can just worry about how you'd like to make love."

He let out a long, unsteady breath as the sheet fell away, leaving him standing naked while Cordelia ran her hands freely all over him. He was magnificent—all hard muscle and sinew covered by a golden tan. And judging by the look in his eye, he was not completely convinced by his own argument. Crash looked highly seducible.

She lifted her mouth to his and murmured, "We're alone now. Wouldn't you like to..."

His warm gaze didn't waver from hers. "Oh, I'd like to, all right."

"You don't sound very enthusiastic."

"I'm trying to be logical."

"Would this make you less logical?"

She touched Crash intimately, her fingertips discovering he was already hard and ready. She played a feathery game with the length of him and heard Crash suck in a tense breath. Her own heart suddenly began to thump.

Crash stood very still and decided he would carry her into the bedroom and have his way with her in the next two minutes, if he really wanted to. And parts of him *really* wanted to.

But a voice was nagging in the back of his head. A very stern, logical voice.

"Hold it," he said, amazing himself.

"Hold what? This?"

"I didn't mean that! I just— Oh, boy."

"Do you like this?"

"Slim," he began, but the protest sounded feeble even to his own ears. All sensible thought suddenly seemed very difficult.

Cordelia smiled shyly up at him. "I've never touched a man like this before. It's very—exciting, isn't it?"

"Just be careful. I'm not—I can't—"

"Does this feel good?"

It felt better than good. Crash closed his eyes and gave up trying to resist. Gentle, yet insistent, Cordelia's touch became rhythmic and delicious. Then she stretched on tiptoe and melted her lips against his. Her tongue flicked out teasingly. Crash was on fire in seconds. He found himself holding her shoulders and crushing Cordelia closer, closer.

She whispered, "Let's go to bed."

"Is it far?"

"A few steps."

"Too far," he muttered, filling his hands with her breasts and groaning when she increased the tempo of her caresses. Hot lava boiled inside him and threatened to explode at any second.

"Touch me," Cordelia breathed in his ear. "Touch me everywhere."

"If...if I do," he growled, "I won't be able to stop."

"I feel how hard you are, Crash. You want me, too."

"You bet," he rasped, grinding his teeth. "But this isn't right, Slim."

"Am I doing something wrong?"

Her hand faltered, but Crash covered her hand with his and quickly reestablished the slow, erotic rhythm. He even started to move his hips to make it better. "No, that's right. It's very right. I meant with your family. Maybe we'd better stop and think. No—don't stop yet. Oh, man."

"Do you like this?"

"Slim—"

"Harder?"

"Oh, *man*—"

"Faster?"

He groaned, unable to speak.

"Listen to me, Crash. We both want this. I need you, and you want to be with me. It's simple. Very simple." She untied the ribbons on her gown and pressed her bare breasts against his chest. Her breath had turned to panting, and her green eyes were afire with desire. "Just do it, Crash. Help me."

But the best way he could help her, Crash knew, was to stop. He barely knew what he was doing, but he seized her wrist and halted the exquisite caresses. She caught her breath and stepped back, looking beautiful with her gown slipping off her shoulders and her throat pulsing with excitement.

"I can't," he said.

Her expression changed in a blink—from passionate to furious. "Yes, you can!"

"All right, on one condition!"

"You have no right to set conditions!"

He tightened his grip on her wrist to quell her. "Do you want this or not?"

"All right, all right. What condition?"

"That you go out with me tonight first."

"Out?" Her brows came down with a rush. "Out where?"

"Into the city. We'll get some kind of disguise for you and sneak out for a few hours."

"Where? Why?"

"It doesn't matter where. I just want you to get your mind off your problem for a little while. We'll relax. And when we come back, if you still want to go through with this—"

"I *will!*"

"*If* you do, we'll make love as many times as you like."

Her eyes were narrow with anger. "Promise?"

"I promise."

Standing with the waning evening light pouring down over her white breasts, she looked like a goddess in a painting. A pregnant goddess of spring, Crash thought foolishly. Beautiful and womanly and full of life. She made no effort to cover herself, and neither did Crash. They simply stared at each other and felt the air crackle with tension.

Damn it, I better not be falling for her, Crash thought suddenly. But she was lovely and vulnerable and passionate and—just about everything any man could appreciate most in a woman.

But her voice was cold as she straightened and said, "All right, it's a deal. But as soon as we're finished in bed, Mr. Craddock," she continued, her voice trembling with anger, "I'm sending you back to your sunken boat, and you can go back to giving orders to waitresses again."

"Don't be angry."

"Why not? I know what I want! You're treating me like a child!"

"I'm treating you the best way I know how, Slim."

Eight

Sneaking out of the palace wasn't hard. Cordelia had done it before during her teenage years. The secret tunnel—first used during the Resistance movement during World War II and later by three adventurous teenage princesses—was dark and full of cobwebs, but with Crash there to negotiate the spiders and creaky gates at either end of the passage, the trip wasn't bad.

Before leaving the palace, Cordelia had allowed Crash to choose her disguise. He ordered her into the maternity sundress she'd worn when they'd first met, combined with a black scoop-necked ballet shirt underneath, old sneakers and a mismatched cardigan sweater over it all. With her distinctive black hair in a careless ponytail, no makeup and her reading glasses perched on her nose, Cordelia hardly looked like a glamorous princess anymore.

Crash had climbed back into his newly washed jeans, then added a clean shirt and a baseball cap dragged from his duffel bag. With no shave, he had a slightly piratelike air as he swung Cordelia over a wooden barricade that blocked the entrance to the tunnel.

An hour later they emerged from the other end of the labyrinthine tunnel and wound their way down the narrow, cobblestoned streets of Cordofino to the center of the ancient city.

"What's all the excitement about?" Crash asked as they took note of banners, flags and paper lights strung overhead. From the streets below rose a cacophony of music—several kinds of bands all playing at once.

"Today is the first day of the wine-making festival."

"Oh, yeah?"

"It's an ancient celebration," Cordelia explained, feeling her spirits rise. "As old as Cordofino. In modern times, of course, my family has combined it with a few other Cordofinian customs—the charity golf tournament and a celebrity tennis match, for example."

Crash leaned over a parapet to look down on the golden streets and pink tile rooftops below. "Sounds pretty festive, all right."

Cordelia followed him and looked down over the city she had always loved. It was colorful and full of music as the sun set over its ancient hillside buildings. "My father likes raising money for charities, and events like these are good advertising for Cordofino. We rely on tourism, you see."

"What are you going to show me first?"

"What?"

Crash turned around and leaned on the edge of the parapet, arms folded over his chest. "I want to look around your city. Where should we go first?"

"I'm not a tour guide!"

"What's the matter?" he taunted with a grin. "Don't you know the best restaurants? The friendliest bar? The prettiest park to go necking with your boyfriend?"

"I don't have boyfriends, remember? And I—I'm not very familiar with the city, to tell the truth. Just the casinos and the buildings we use for royal functions."

"You're kidding." He looked genuinely surprised. "You never went exploring?"

"Of course we did! I could find the way to my father's stable with my eyes closed. We used to sneak down there frequently to see the horses when I was young."

Crash made a face. "I'd rather see people than horses tonight. Besides, I'm starving."

"You just ate four watercress sandwiches!"

"You call that food?" He pushed off the parapet, linked his arm with Cordelia's and drew her down the street. "First we'll have dinner and then— Hold it." He stopped dead. "I don't suppose you have any cash on you?"

"Cash?" she repeated weakly.

"Money. We won't get very far if we're broke."

"I never learned to carry money. Oh, I'm sorry!" Sweetly she said, "I guess we'll have to turn back, won't we?"

"Oh, no, you don't !" Crash groped in his pockets and came up with a few tattered bills that had obviously been through the laundry. He sighed. "American money—twelve dollars."

Cordelia bit her lower lip, not sure whether she wanted to go ahead with the adventure or run back to her nice, safe apartment in the palace. Then she found herself shyly saying, "Our country uses all currencies. It's the only way Cordofino could survive. We won't have any trouble spending American dollars."

He cocked an amused eyebrow at her. "We'll have trouble finding a decent meal for twelve measly bucks, I'm afraid."

An idea occurred to Cordelia. "Let's go to the casino. We can win more money!"

With a laugh, Crash took her arm again. "Guys like me don't win money at casinos, Slim. We're the ones who make gambling so profitable for your family. Besides, they'll never let us into a casino dressed as we are."

"Nonsense," Cordelia said. "I'm a princess!"

"Not tonight, you aren't. Tonight, you're a commoner." He pulled her into the street. "C'mon. We'll have a good time on a budget."

Cordelia's spirits rose even higher as they hurried down the cobblestones toward the music and aromatic air of the city's central square. Crash's good humor was infectious. As they got farther from the palace, crowds of happy citizens and flush-faced tourists thronged the narrow streets. Crash and Cordelia turned a corner and came upon a tuba band playing German polkas. An elderly couple dressed in traditional Cordofinian costume danced for the enjoyment of the crowd. On the next street, a quartet of violinists entertained another group with spirited renditions of Mozart pieces.

Along that street, a local tavern had set up a series of long tables and covered them with white linens. Lined on the tables were samples of wine in plastic cups, with dozens of bottles for sale.

Crash immediately befriended the tipsy tavern owner, and together they sampled several varieties of wine, laughing and joking together. Cordelia hung back, afraid she would be recognized and immediately mobbed. But the tavern owner barely gave her a glance—except to approvingly pat her belly and then throw his arm around Crash's shoulders in a congratulatory slap. "I wish you many sons and daughters, my friend!"

Cordelia blushed to think the tavern owner believed her to be Crash's wife, but Crash laughed and pretended nothing was amiss as he accepted another cupful of the wine.

"Have a sip?" he asked Cordelia, offering her the cup.

"No, thank you."

"What's this?" he inquired, feigning surprise. "A sudden concern for our baby's health?"

"Nothing of the sort! I just think one of us should keep our head."

"Come on. Let yourself have a little fun."

"Don't you think I know how to have fun?" Cordelia snatched the cup from Crash and took a fierce sip of the robust red wine. Its heady bouquet burst on her tongue.

"Like it?" Crash asked.

"It's okay," she replied. "A little rustic. Untamed, perhaps, but—"

"Oh, spare me the highbrow palace baloney!" He laughed, his dark eyes alight. "Do you like it or not?"

"I like it," Cordelia said at last, and she risked a smile.

He returned her smile with one that unnerved Cordelia with its warmth. "Good. Now, let's see what else we can get for free."

He took her hand and led Cordelia into the crowd. A group of shrieking children ran by, clutching sparklers that danced like colorful fireflies over their heads. Their indulgent parents—a group of friends clearly out for an evening's stroll—laughed and talked together on the street corner.

Seeing them, Cordelia felt a pang of regret. All around her was the evidence of her own sheltered life. People were having a wonderful time—in couples, in small groups, in crowds. Together. Not alone.

"What's wrong?" Crash asked when her silence became obvious.

"Nothing. I-it's nothing." She was surprised that he'd noticed her change of mood.

"Don't tell me it's nothing. What are you thinking?"

"You wouldn't understand."

Crash accepted an orange offered by a friendly fruit stand owner, who smiled and bowed as they passed him. Crash called his thanks, then began to peel the orange and said, "Try me."

At one of the outdoor cafés, another group of festival-goers burst into singing. As they merrily bawled a German drinking song, Cordelia said softly, "I've never done this before."

"Mingled with the peasantry, you mean?"

"Not like this, not as one of them. Usually I'm—"

"Usually you're dressed in your finery while everybody smiles and bows to you? But nobody gets friendly, do they?"

"No, they don't. Even now, I can't... Oh, I don't know."

"Relax. Nobody's going to guess who you are. Not looking like this." He plucked at her cardigan sweater and laughed.

"Are you saying I look like a scullery maid?" Cordelia demanded, unable to prevent a smile of her own.

"Yes," he promptly replied. "But a very beautiful scullery maid."

He bent swiftly and kissed her on the mouth. His lips lingered warmly on Cordelia's, making her head swim with pleasure. And something else—something she couldn't put a name to. It felt like a stirring emotion. For a moment the music and noise receded, and all Cordelia knew was Crash. She wanted to throw her arms around his neck and kiss him all night long, to be with him, to hold him and talk to him and be his friend.

Nearby a group of people responded by applauding their public display of affection. Cordelia blushed and pulled away, but Crash laughed and sketched a melodramatic bow to his audience. They laughed, too, and raised their glasses in a toast.

Then they walked on, and Crash finished peeling the orange, whistling. He passed a section to Cordelia without speaking, and she ate his offering hungrily. It didn't blend well with the vestiges of the wine, but Cordelia decided that was the flavor of the evening— a blend of the sweet and pungent, the piquant and simple. Either that, or she was getting a little drunk.

A juggler appeared on the next street, and the crowd that gathered around him shouted and applauded his skills. They joined the crowd for a while, eating the orange and laughing with everyone else when the juggler snatched Crash's hat and combined it into his act. When the hat was returned, they moved along.

Down a side street, a marimba band was making a joyful noise on their steel drums. The intense rhythm drew them closer and soon had Crash dancing as they pressed through the throng. He tossed the remaining orange peel into a trash barrel and grabbed Cordelia's hands. They danced together, and Cordelia found herself filled with delight as she watched Crash's face—his smile, his laughing dark eyes, the wild lock of hair that kept brushing his forehead.

He pulled her close and they moved in deliciously sinuous syncopation. Although Cordelia had to turn slightly sideways to accommodate her belly, he managed to make the contact between their bodies complete. Crash's lean hips were supple, his arms gentle as he held her. Although other dancers crowded close, Cordelia felt safe in Crash's arms as they danced.

It wasn't just music that moved them. There was something new beating in Cordelia's veins. She was sure Crash felt it, too.

Cheek to cheek, he put his mouth next to her ear. "Hungry yet?"

She didn't pull away. "Not yet."

"Telling the truth?"

She laughed against his cheek and slipped her fingers into his hair. "I'm starving, actually. But I don't want this to end."

"The music will be here all night. We'll come back."

"Then I'm famished."

"This way."

He pulled her out from among the dancing couples and back to the square. All the restaurants were jammed with patrons, so it took half an hour's wandering to find the right place to fit their budget.

At last Crash found a table for them in one of the crowded outdoor cafés. A harried waiter led them through a maze of tables under a green-and-white striped awning. A hundred noisy patrons made an awful racket around them—some singing, some shouting greetings to each other, some just trying to make conversation over the din. The chef had wheeled a cart out from the kitchen, and he set fire to a dish. With a flourishing bow, he served the flambé to an applauding table.

Their waiter seated Crash and Cordelia at a small table near the street and gave them menus.

"What are you in the mood for?" Crash asked.

"I'd love a glass of champagne right now."

"Sorry, Slim. Champagne isn't in our budget tonight. We'll have a couple of draft beers," he told the waiter. "And some of that melted cheese stuff." He pointed to another table, where a couple seemed engrossed in swirling bits of bread in a potful of fragrant cheese. Raclette was a traditional Cordofinian dish. The waiter scribbled their order and rushed away to comply. Then, putting his elbows on the small table and leaning toward her, Crash said, "I hope that's okay. For the baby, I mean."

"The doctor I was seeing on St. Bart's said I could have a little alcohol now and then."

Crash raised his brows. "What were you doing on St. Barthelémy Island?"

"My family keeps a summer house there. That's where I've been hiding ever since...well, ever since the baby."

"So you could keep your condition a secret from the press."

Cordelia nodded. "And my family. I had to stay out of sight until I knew I couldn't be convinced to get rid of the baby. I saw a doctor regularly and spent most of my time taking care of myself."

"You've done a good job," Crash remarked with a smile, slowly reaching out one finger to slide a curl of her hair back from her temples.

Cordelia saw that he was completely sincere, and she smiled, despite the rush of odd nervousness that went through her veins. "Thank you."

"Are you going back to the island to deliver the baby?"

"Oh, no. Now that I'm here, I'll have to stay. The doctor was nervous about my traveling this late in my pregnancy."

Crash frowned. "Why?"

"I might have the baby early."

"Really? He said that?" Crash's gaze darkened and automatically traveled to her belly. "Should we go back to the palace? I never thought—"

"I'm fine."

"But—" Crash looked disconcerted. "Do you have a doctor here? How will you . . . ? I mean—"

"My family has two full-time physicians. I'm sure one of them can take care of me when the time comes."

"Are you practicing all the breathing and exercises?"

"Heavens, no." The waiter appeared with two glasses foaming with beer, and Cordelia waited while he set them on the table and departed. Then she picked up her glass and said, "I intend to demand every drug known to mankind and wake up when it's all over."

"That's pretty unusual these days," Crash observed. He lifted his glass, too, but didn't drink. "Are you sure that's best for the baby?"

Cordelia sipped her beer and found it crisp and cool in her throat. "I don't care, really."

"That's not true," Crash said with conviction.

Feeling herself color, Cordelia said, "I don't. As you know, my reasons for doing this were never traditional. I want out of the life my parents want for me, and this was the only surefire way I could see to do that."

"But you must think about it," Crash pressed. "About having a baby. About being a mother."

She laughed shortly. "You said yourself, I hardly look like the motherly type."

"Maybe I was wrong," Crash said. He drank off the top two inches of his beer, then set the glass down, still studying Cordelia. "Before, I couldn't imagine it, but now... well, I think you're probably capable of doing anything you set your mind to."

"Well, I've set my mind to hiring a good nanny."

"So you can run off and have fun?" Crash shook his head. "I don't see you doing that. Angelique probably could. And I think Julianna would make a better Nazi than a mother. But you—I think you're going to change your mind."

"You don't know me very well."

"I think I do." Crash held her gaze for a long moment. "You're scared, aren't you?"

"Of childbirth? Isn't every woman?"

"It's not just that, though, is it? It's the part that comes after."

Cordelia managed a smile and ran her fingertips down the condensation on the sides of her glass. "I come from a long line of terrible mothers."

"That doesn't mean you will be."

She glanced away. "Look, I've never been especially successful at anything I've ever tried."

"That's nonsense."

"No, I'm a C student in everything—average, but not great."

"You're not stupid, Slim. I saw those letters you wrote this afternoon, and I've seen you handle people. You're highly skilled, but you don't recognize it." He leaned closer. "Now here's a chance to be great at mothering. You can do it."

"Even I know it's foolish to start out climbing mountains when a few hikes in the woods would be the sensible starting place."

"You *are* scared, aren't you?"

Cordelia looked down into her beer. Her fists were tight on the tabletop. Strangely, she found herself admitting the truth. "I just don't want to ruin this child's life."

"Slim—"

"No, I've been pretty screwed up myself thanks to poor parenting, and I—I just don't want to risk— Oh, damn, I don't know what I want. Why are you making me say these things?"

"You need to get them off your chest, don't you?" Crash covered her hand with his.

"I don't know what to think," Cordelia said, amazed to find herself trembling. "I know I was reckless. I saw a chance and I took it without thinking things through very carefully. And now..."

"There's no turning back," Crash said softly.

"No. And soon there's going to be someone other than myself to think about."

"Babies are pretty tough. They don't need much."

"But I'm such a self-centered fool—you said so yourself!"

"I did?"

"Well, you should have!" Cordelia snapped. "I don't think I have what it takes."

"You have time, don't you?"

"What do you mean?"

Crash cradled her hand in his, toying with her fingertips soothingly. "I haven't told you much about myself," he began. "I spent some pretty messed up years with my mother, but I never really had a family until I went to live with her friends in Texas. Bonnie and Joe Parsons. They became my family—Bonnie and Joe and their five kids. All five of them younger than me."

Cordelia saw Crash's face soften as he remembered his past. With a hint of a self-deprecating grin, he continued. "I helped take care of them all. Even little Crystal, when she was born. In a big family, everybody has to pitch in and help do everything, so I learned how to change diapers and warm bottles—the whole nine yards. And if I could do it at age sixteen, Slim, you can do it now."

"But—"

His hand tightened on hers. "All it takes is time. Babies need to be held and talked to and fed regularly, but mostly they just want to be around people. Around their families."

"I'm just one person."

"Sometimes that's enough."

She couldn't help a wry smile. "Are you suggesting I have another one soon?"

He smiled, too. "Sure. Big families are a lot of fun."

"Crash..."

"Yeah?"

Cordelia wanted to ask him questions. A lot of questions that had to do with babies, but even more than that had to do with just him. Mostly, she wanted to ask him to stay with her. To be with her for those first few weeks when she'd be all thumbs with her child. Crash was someone she could depend on. Someone she could talk to and admit her fears to.

Someone she could trust.

Before she could find the words to say what was in her heart, the waiter arrived. He brought a large tray laden with a basket of bread and fruit chunks and a hot bowl of raclette.

Crash thought Cordelia had never looked so beautiful as she did just before the waiter interrupted. Behind her reading glasses, her green eyes shone with emotion—emotion as he'd never seen in her before. And Crash found himself thinking how lucky any kid would be to wake up every morning with that face bending over his crib.

She blushed and thanked the waiter, who bowed and lit the candle in the middle of their table before retreating, leaving them alone with their food.

Crash shook himself out of his reverie and poked at the bread basket. "How do we eat this stuff, anyway?"

Cordelia picked up one of the long-handled forks and explained how to go about dipping the bread and fruit into the melted cheese. Crash didn't listen to a word but watched her agile fingers as they maneuvered the fork. He listened to the musical rise and fall of her voice, looked deeply into those fathomless green eyes and wondered what the hell he was doing.

Why wasn't he whisking her off to some desert paradise where they could live out their days and nights together, making more babies until they were hip deep in kids?

Why wasn't he carrying her straight back to that pretty bedroom in the palace and making long, crazy love to her right now?

Cordelia extended her fork to him, and Crash opened his mouth to take the raclette. It might have been poison, but it tasted like the most delicious food he'd ever eaten in his life—all because it was Cordelia's face he stared into through the flickering candlelight.

"Now you try," she coaxed, forcing Crash to wake up and try to feed himself.

He fumbled with the fork, but managed to eat more than his share of the melted cheese while Cordelia watched and laughed at his clumsiness.

"Tell me more about your childhood," she said as the twilight gathered around them.

Fortunately, Crash had his mouth full, which gave him a full minute to think through a response.

"Oh, there's not much more than I told you already."

"What about Texas? Did you live on a ranch?"

"Nope. A big house on the college campus. The Parsons were both professors."

"And you went to college there, too?"

"On a football scholarship and money I made painting houses, tending bar, helping out on fishing boats—"

She smiled. "You're a man of many talents."

"But a master of none, I'm afraid. Like you, I haven't found what I want to do with the rest of my life. Mostly, I know what I *don't* want to do."

"Like what?"

"Wearing a suit and tie. Going to work, nine to five every day in some stuffy office. I don't mind being broke as long as I don't have to butter up the boss."

With a laugh, Cordelia said, "You'd make a good king!"

Crash choked on an apple slice. "What?"

She leaned one elbow on the table, placing her chin in her cupped palm. "You sounded like my father for a minute. He hates answering to anyone, and he wants to schedule his own time. He refuses to have a secretary. He says it would stifle him to have someone else in charge of his affairs. Mind you, he works very hard and he's passionate about certain causes, but he's... well, he definitely likes to be the boss."

"He's got a lot of responsibilities."

"Oh, yes, a great many. But he doesn't mind those. I guess that's what it means to be born noble."

"You were born noble."

"Not like my father."

Crash chewed thoughtfully. "I know what you mean."

"Do you?"

"Not myself, of course. I was never meant to be the least bit useful."

She eyed him over the candle for a moment. "I don't know about that."

The group of strolling tuba players appeared in the street near the café then, and their music drowned out any further conversation. Cordelia turned to watch the musicians play, and Crash studied her classic profile in the evening light while thinking about a future that might have been.

The waiter soon cleared their table and brought coffee, which they drank while the musicians played a noisy selection of popular tunes and polkas on their tubas. Cordelia laughed and clapped along with the other café patrons.

Then the night sky was suddenly filled with a burst of fireworks. Everyone oohed and aahed, and began to applaud.

"The annual fireworks display," Cordelia explained. "To start the festival. They're really wonderful!"

"Should we go back to the palace to watch? I'm sure the best view is up there."

She bit her lip and looked at Crash with hope gleaming in her eyes. "We don't have to go back yet, do we?"

He felt his heart soften. "Of course not."

"Let's go out to the park."

Crash paid the bill—less than eight dollars—and left the rest of his cash as a tip for the waiter. Then he pulled Cordelia out of the restaurant.

She paused in the doorway, though, and put her hand on her belly. "Crash—wait."

He hurried back to her side. "Are you okay?"

"I think so. But the baby—"

A clutch of fear seized his chest. "I'll call a taxi. We'd better get you back home."

"No, please." She put her hand on his chest. As if dizzy, she removed her glasses and tucked them into her pocket. "It's just a kick."

The owner of the restaurant appeared in the doorway, sensing trouble. "Can I help, *monsieur?*"

"Yes, the prin—I mean, this young lady isn't feeling well."

"I'm fine," she insisted. "It was just a twinge."

A frown deepened on the face of the restaurant owner. "Perhaps *madam* would like to rest somewhere quiet?"

"Just for a moment, yes."

"This way."

The gentleman led the way back through his restaurant to the kitchen. With Crash and Cordelia just a step behind, he guided them through the fragrant steam that billowed from the stoves, then out through a rear door.

"Here," he said, casting his arm wide to indicate a small private garden. "It is quiet here, and *madam* can watch the fireworks in peace."

"Thank you," Cordelia murmured, glancing around the small, exquisitely tended garden and looking touched. "This is very kind."

"Not at all," the restaurant owner said, bowing. Then, to Crash, he said, "If you need help, just knock on this door. Someone will come at once."

"Thanks."

The owner left them, closing the kitchen door and leaving the garden in darkness. Except for the moon and stars overhead, the small paradise was puddled with dark shapes beneath a spreading elm tree. Then another burst of fireworks lit up the sky, and Cordelia cried out with pleasure. "Oh, look!"

"Let's sit down," Crash commanded, taking her hand. He led her to a set of circular wrought-iron steps that wound up the side of the restaurant. "You should rest awhile."

"I'm fine, Crash, really."

"Indulge me," he replied.

With a tolerant sigh, she sat down on the second step and slid over to make room for Crash beside her. He leaned back against the railing, turned sideways and pulled Cordelia back against him so they could look at the fireworks together. With her head on his chest, her hair spilling across his shoulder in the moonlight, Crash wrapped his arms around her to keep her warm. His hands met just above the baby.

After a shy moment, she covered his hands with hers. Then Crash felt the baby move—a soft surge of life that made him catch his breath.

"Wow," he said, stunned. "Does that happen often?"

"A hundred times a day," she said with a laugh. "And around this time of night, she does a whole trapeze routine just before falling asleep."

"She?"

"Well..." Cordelia hesitated. "Until lately, I just assumed it would be a girl."

"But now?"

"I— Oh, look!"

They sat together for a long time, watching the fireworks overhead and feeling the baby play inside Cordelia. Gradually the child gave up kicking, though, and Crash drowsily caressed Cordelia as the sky burst with color and light.

"Oh, Crash," she sighed. "Tonight has been a wonderful adventure."

"Do you like being a commoner?"

"With you, yes."

Relaxed against him, she felt warm and sensual. Beneath his gently massaging hands, the baby seemed to go to sleep.

Safe in the darkness, intoxicated by the scents of flowers, Crash felt bold enough to touch her even more intimately. Slowly he let his hands roam over Cordelia—drawing slow circles around her breasts and even massaging her thighs with slow, exploring hands. Her nipples grew hard under his touch, and her thighs loosened when he stroked them.

The music in the street sounded distant, but the tempo of Cordelia's breathing matched the beat.

"Crash," she began.

"Ready to leave?"

"No. Not yet." She twisted in his arms and suddenly lay on his chest, her face upturned to the starlight. "Will you kiss me?"

"Like this?" He kissed her forehead, then her nose, then her cheek.

"No. Like you mean it." Her eyes were solemnly beautiful, radiating a vulnerability that tugged at Crash's heartstrings.

"I do mean it," he said roughly, and pulled her face close between his hands. He took her mouth with his, savoring her lips, breathing in her scent, cupping her face as if it were the most fragile bone china.

She wrapped her arms around his neck and pressed closer still. She must have felt his immediate arousal, because she rode gently against its heat. Their lips parted, their tongues met, their breath mingled in a single, shaky inhalation.

Cordelia sighed and held him close as the kiss deepened. Crash thought he might happily drown in her. She fired everything that was exciting and yet tender in him. She was a woman like he'd never known—one who could inflame and enthrall.

Before he knew what she was doing, Cordelia had unfastened his belt and his jeans. When she touched his arousal with her fingertips a moment later, Crash thought he might explode at once.

"Wait," he said, and struggled to grab her wrist.

"I can't," she whispered, caressing him. "This is right."

"Not now. Cordelia, wait."

She slid out of her panties and then straddled Crash as he sat on the step. With her knees on either side of his hips, she trapped him there. Then she slid one hand around the nape of his neck and played her fingers in his hair. Her lips touched his again, smiling. "Now," she whispered. "Like this."

Common sense ordered Crash to stop. But she was irresistible. In a heartbeat, Crash was out of his jeans. He wrapped both arms around her and kissed her deeply. Then Cordelia pressed her hands against his chest and let out a long, long breath as she sank down upon him.

She was tight—too tight, he thought at first, but also warm and liquid. Instinctively, Crash held still while Cordelia slowly, slowly let him inside. His heart hammered in his chest. A riot of protests ricocheted in his head.

But in time, he was hard and deep within her, and there was no going back.

Cordelia released a taut breath. "Oh, Crash."

"You're a fool, Cordelia."

"I know, I know. But this is right, isn't it?" Her green eyes were wide on his, yet clouded with desire. "It's not a business arrangement, is it?"

"No, love. It's not that."

"It's better this way."

"Much better."

He slid his hands under her dress and grasped her hips. She gasped.

"Am I hurting you?"

"No, no. It's good. Show me more."

So he took her there on the steps. Like a couple of teenagers, they rocked and thrust and made hot, sweet love under the blaze of festival fireworks. Crash climaxed inside her and held Cordelia in his arms for a long time afterward, kissing, nibbling and whispering nonsense until the world stopped spinning like a crazy top.

He was in love with her. There was no denying that. But it would have been stupid to tell her. Stupid to think it might all work out after all. Crash felt his heart turn over as he held Cordelia in his arms, listening to her breathe.

"Crash?"

"Cordelia."

"I wish— Oh, God, I wish a lot of things."

He hugged her close, eyes shut tight. "Me, too, love. Me, too."

There was nothing more to say, Crash knew. It was impossible. She had a life to live that was so utterly different from his that it was ridiculous.

The night sky darkened, and Cordelia and Crash fixed their clothes.

Just in time.

The kitchen door burst back on its hinges and their paradise was invaded by storm troopers from the palace. Cordelia cried out.

With Rudi breathing fire in the lead, the guards dragged Cordelia out of Crash's arms.

"Rudi! What's the meaning of this? Stop it!"

"Orders from the palace, Your Highness."

She fought to escape the restraining hands of the guards, while Crash was seized and dragged off the stairs by a hard-breathing Rudi and two of his fellow thugs.

"Rudi, stop! This is my private business and nothing to be interfered with! *Rudi!*"

"It's okay, Slim."

"No, it's not! I won't— Oh, my God!"

Crash tried to shrug out of his captor's grasp but succeeded only in enraging everybody. Exasperated, Rudi swung a lucky punch. Crash saw it coming, but there was no time to duck. His head snapped back, and he felt a swirl of darkness rush up around him as the pain exploded in his cheekbone. Cordelia's voice— a high, thin cry—was the last thing he remembered.

An hour later Crash woke up and heard they'd taken her back to the palace in a limousine.

Nine

———

"Mama, I can't believe you actually called out the troops!"

"Cordelia, dear, it's for your own good."

As morning light streamed in through her bedroom window, Cordelia dressed as quickly as she could. "You mean for *your* own good! How could you humiliate me like that! What a public spectacle! The whole festival came to a complete stop to see me wrestled into that car!"

"Just get dressed, dear. And hurry. Your father's demanding to see you at once."

Angelique, lazily reclining in one of the wing chairs near Cordelia's bed, said, "Are you sure this is wise, Mama? Cordelia doesn't look so hot this morning. Are you feeling all right, Sis?"

"Since when does anybody care about how I feel?"

But Angelique did have a frown of concern on her face. "Maybe you should just go back to bed and take it easy."

"I'm fine," Cordelia snapped. "I just want to know where Crash is."

"You'll see Charles in good time, dear." Geraldine helped Cordelia into her sweater.

"Is he all right? You haven't hurt him, have you? Mama, please tell me the truth! If you've locked him in the cellar again—"

"Calm yourself, Cordelia."

But Princess Geraldine looked anything but calm herself. Her Royal Majesty paced the bedroom frantically, wringing her hands.

Cordelia had hustled into one of her many cashmere maternity sweaters and a pair of white, wool, elastic-waist trousers. With surprise, she realized the waistband was almost too snug for comfort. In just a week's time, her size had grown. She took no time to change into something better fitting, but hastily brushed her hair and pronounced herself ready for the early morning audience.

Cordelia was surprised again when her mother and sister escorted her to the throne room, one of the few formal rooms the family ever made use of for private audiences.

"Papa must have something big up his sleeve," she muttered as they entered through a pair of oak doors that had been carved in the fifteenth century.

The massive, echoing chamber, decorated with flags and gilt furniture, was unpopulated except for one impassive steward and Prince Henri, who sat majestically on his throne and looked up from a sheaf of papers to watch Cordelia's approach with an imperi-

ously cold expression on his stern face. He wore a
plain blue business suit—his customary attire during
the daylight hours—with the traditional royal sash
draped across one shoulder. The red velvet sash was
decorated with assorted ribbons and medals that
glinted by the light of four fully illuminated crystal
chandeliers.

"You've gone to a lot of trouble, Papa," Cordelia
said as she arrived in front of his throne. "You must
have a bombshell to drop. Am I going to be burned at
the stake?"

"Nothing of the kind," replied Prince Henri, his
voice betraying no emotion. He put the sheaf of papers down on one knee. Beside him, the royal steward
didn't move a muscle as the prince said, "I'm wel-
coming you back into the family, Cordelia."

"What?"

"And your child, too, I suppose."

"What are you talking about, Papa?"

"I believe," said the prince, "we have reached the
decision that you may remain first in line for the royal
succession despite your, er, condition."

Cordelia felt weak. "You've changed the law?"

"Certainly not," he said crisply. "The law remains
the same. A daughter of the royal house may not
marry anyone but a royal prince. To preserve the
blood, to ensure Cordofino's future—"

"Oh, baloney, Papa! It's a stupid law, and you
know it!"

"Nevertheless, it is a law of this land, and I will
fight to preserve it."

"But I've already slept with a commoner, Papa.
Remember? And here's the proof!"

Prince Henri eyed her belly with distaste, but shook his head. "You can't deceive us any longer, Cordelia."

"You think I've got a pillow under this sweater? Come put your hand on me and you'll feel—"

"I have just received," he interrupted her, lifting the papers, "correspondence confirming your mother's theory about the child's conception. These letters come from something called a woman's health clinic in New Jersey, U.S.A."

"But—"

"The director of the clinic was unwilling, at first, to give us any information. But you know, Cordelia, our family is capable of applying all sorts of pressure. I donated a hefty sum to your clinic, and by twisting a few arms, my agents obtained the information we needed."

Cordelia felt faint. Prickles of heat sprang out on her brow. "You didn't! They can't—they promised—"

Prince Henri's voice swept on. "The director of the clinic tells me that your child was not conceived in the, er, natural manner, Cordelia. You were artificially impregnated."

"All right, all right!" she cried. "I *was* inseminated artificially, but since then I—we've slept together."

The prince regarded her with disdain. "You're lying, young lady."

"I'm not! Crash and I have made love."

The prince colored, perhaps because his steward made a small choking noise in the back of his throat. But Henri recovered and said coldly, "The Ladies of the Bedchamber claim there has been no evidence of such a union.''

''Well, they're wrong!''

''They are the official referees in this situation, Cordelia.''

''You take their word over mine? Your daughter's lying and that's that?'' Cordelia swayed unsteadily on her feet. ''I won't stand for it, Papa! Ask Crash. Ask him, and he'll back me up. You can fight both of us!''

The prince turned to his steward. ''Bring in the prisoner.''

''Prisoner!'' Cordelia gasped. ''Papa, you didn't!''

''If you can't keep your voice down, this audience is over.''

Cordelia desperately wanted to sit down, for her knees felt as if they might give at any moment. But there was no chair nearby—her father's design, no doubt—so she stayed on her feet and willed herself not to collapse during the three minutes it took the steward to depart and return with Crash.

Cordelia almost ran into his arms. He looked haggard, unshaven and rumpled—another night spent in his clothes, Cordelia thought with a surge of sympathy. Then she saw the bruise on his cheekbone, and she was suddenly furious.

''Papa, this isn't the Middle Ages! You can't treat people like they're animals! You can't even treat *animals* the way you've— Oh, Crash, are you all right? Please, I never thought you'd be—''

''It's okay, Princess.'' Crash caught her arms firmly and held her. Soothingly he said, ''Take it easy, will you? I'm fine. But you— Damn, you're shaking like a leaf.''

"I'm fine. Just upset." She touched her fingertips to the angry bruise on his face. "Crash, please forgive my family for the way you've been treated."

Prince Henri interrupted again. "Don't apologize for anyone but yourself, Cordelia. You and this man have conspired to defraud us—"

Cordelia turned to face her father. "Crash didn't conspire to do anything! I forced him to come with me—"

"Who forced whom?" the prince asked.

"*I* made Crash come with me, Papa."

"Perhaps he took advantage of you, Cordelia."

"That's nonsense. I instigated everything, Papa."

In a drawl, Crash said, "Well, that's not exactly true, is it, Princess?"

"Please, Crash, don't say anything that could—"

Sharply, the prince snapped, "Are you admitting that you had relations with my daughter, Mr. Craddock?"

"He did! But it wasn't against my will. I was the one—"

"Let him answer for himself, Cordelia. Mr. Craddock?"

Cordelia spun around and grasped Crash's shirt in her clenched hands. "Don't say a word, Crash. They'll have you arrested. Just let me take the blame."

Without moving from his throne, Henri said sternly, "There will be no question of taking blame or being arrested. My goal is to finish this business as quickly as possible and put it behind us. To that end, Mr. Craddock, I am prepared to send you back to your own country and pay you a small sum of money to ensure your silence in this matter."

"Papa!"

"Be quiet, Cordelia. I am making your friend a simple offer."

"You're twisting everything around. You're blackmailing him, Papa. If he doesn't go away, you *will* have him arrested, won't you?"

"Cordelia, if you can't hold your tongue, I will send you to your room. Now, Mr. Craddock, I believe my steward has given you all the facts of the matter. What is your decision?"

Cordelia tipped her face up to Crash's and felt her heart start to pound. In her mind, too many ideas spun crazily around—a confusion of thought and emotion. Mostly emotion. "Crash—"

He looked down at her, and an unmistakably warm flicker of light shone in his dark eyes. "What do you want, Cordelia?" he asked softly.

"I want—I want—"

"You don't know, do you? Not really." He smiled sadly. "You should have thought things through more carefully before you jumped into this crazy plan of yours."

"I don't want to stay here."

"But you belong here."

"No, I don't!"

"You don't belong out in the world. You'd get into too much trouble. It's over, Cordelia."

"Crash, please."

He squeezed her shoulders and looked up at the prince. "Okay, Your Highness. I give up. I never slept with your daughter."

"You're lying!" Cordelia cried.

"No," Crash said. "I'm not."

Cordelia swayed on her feet, her balance maintained only by Crash's embrace. She slumped, resting her forehead on his chest. For an instant she thought she could feel his heart jump.

Then Prince Henri was saying, "Very well, Mr. Craddock. If you renounce all connection to my daughter, we will see that you are returned without delay to your own country."

"Thank you." Crash's voice rasped.

Gently he handed Cordelia into her mother's waiting arms. Cordelia weakly obeyed. She felt hot tears on her cheeks, but she didn't have the strength to dash them away. Nor could she lift her head to meet Crash's gaze again.

Crash said softly, "Take care of yourself, Princess."

Then he was gone.

On his way out of the palace, escorted by two stony-faced guards in the traditional Cordofinian uniforms, Crash tried not to think. *Put one foot in front of the other, Old Man,* he told himself. *Just get out of her life.* He was making the right decision. That much was obvious. What did a mixed-up princess need with a bum like Crash Craddock? *Just go home,* Crash said inwardly. *Don't stop for anything.*

But waiting on the stone staircase at the palace side door, stood Rudi. Crash halted at the sight of Cordelia's bodyguard.

Rudi didn't meet Crash's eye, but held out the duffel bag he had apparently packed with all of Crash's worldly goods. "Here," Rudi said gruffly. "You'll need this stuff."

"Thanks." Crash took the bag. "Listen... Rudi..."

Rudi didn't answer, just nodded.

"You'd better look after her," Crash said unnecessarily. "She needs somebody, you know."

"I know."

"Somebody's got to know what's right for her. She's— Sometimes Cordelia gets ideas in her head... The right choices might be hard for her."

"She's a smart lady. Just mixed up right now."

"Yeah, well, hormones, you know."

"I know."

Crash put out his hand. With just a moment's reluctant hesitation, Rudi took it and they shook hands solemnly. Crash wished he could say a lot more, but suddenly the words got stuck in his throat.

Rudi said, "I'll make sure you get the money she promised you."

"Tell her to keep it."

"She won't. She always keeps her promises."

"I don't give a damn about the money."

"Then," Rudi said slowly, "I'll make sure you get word when... well, when the baby comes."

"Thanks," Crash said shortly. He couldn't say more. Quickly he turned and went down the stone steps to a waiting car.

It wasn't the royal limousine this time, just a plain sedan with a silent driver and a couple of plain-clothed guards wearing mirrored sunglasses. The guards discussed what they intended to have for lunch and seemed totally uninterested in Crash.

Glad to be left alone, Crash took one last look at Cordofino as the car wound its way through the city and out to the airport. He tried not to think. As the car swept past the café where they'd had dinner just a few hours ago, Crash closed his eyes to block out the memories.

Cordelia's jet was waiting on the tarmac at the airport. Crash boarded the aircraft alone, and the guards watched from below as the jet's unsmiling steward greeted Crash, pushed away the gangway and closed the hatch.

Crash found his way to the lounge and sat down in one of the plush seats. He leaned his head back on the cushion and blew a long, unsteady sigh. Damn it, he ought to be happy to be going home—back to the States with a probable million dollars coming to him. What more could a man wish for?

He closed his eyes. *A man can wish for lots of things. Including fairy tales with happy endings.*

Listening to the whine of the engines, Crash couldn't prevent the flood of mental pictures that crowded into his mind. Cordelia the first time she'd stepped out of her car. Cordelia lounging in her bedroom wearing a flowing, flimsy negligee. Cordelia laughing with him in the crowded city streets. And Cordelia lifting her passionate gaze to his, pressing her luscious lips to Crash's hungry mouth, arching her body to better fit his own.

With a groan, Crash tried to block out the images, but they kept rushing into his mind like a relentless surf beating against the ocean shore. The jet took off, yet Crash was barely aware of the aircraft's swift ascent into the sky.

He stood up at last, deciding he might as well go looking for a bed. The days and nights he'd spent in Cordofino hadn't exactly turned out to be restful. Might as well try getting some sleep.

A passageway led from the lounge to a series of closed doors. The first opened into a small bathroom. The second was a private cabin.

Crash let himself in and threw his duffel bag on the floor next to the bed. It was probably the bed Cordelia had slept in when they'd flown across the Atlantic. Crash sat down on the edge of the mattress.

"This is for the best," he said out loud, letting himself fall back onto the bed and staring at the ceiling. "I know that. It's really for the best."

"Whose best?"

"Everybody's," he answered, rubbing his tired face with both hands. "For you, for me. For your country. For— *What the hell?*"

"Hello, Crash."

He sat bolt upright. "Cordelia!"

She stepped out of the closet—beautiful and very real. "Yes, it's me."

Crash fought to control himself, but he was up and grabbing her arms a second later, babbling like a fool. "What are you...? How in hell did you...? Are you *crazy?*"

Cordelia laughed, throwing her head back so she could drink in his face. Her eyes sparkled with light and tears. Her face was white with fear and the first release of tension. "Maybe I am!"

"My God— What have you done?"

"I think it's called stowing away."

"Stowing— Do you mean nobody knows you're here?"

"Rudi does," she said, hugging Crash tight and tucking her head under his chin. "Rudi helped me get away from the palace without being seen. He smuggled me on board with the supplies for the crew. He said we should wait a couple of hours before we let anyone know we were here so they couldn't turn back."

"But—"

"Oh, Crash, just hold me. I'm here with you. Please, hold me."

"Princess, you can't do this." Crash heard himself trying to argue logically, but he couldn't stop squeezing Cordelia snug against his frame. She felt heavenly, smelled delicious, and Crash couldn't make his body behave the way his brain knew it ought to. "My love, you've got to go back."

"No, I can't go back. Not without you, Crash."

"That's nonsense. Your life isn't with me. It's—"

"It's with my baby," she finished, looking at Crash once again. Her gaze glistened with fresh tears, and her lips were trembling. "I'm not making this decision for myself, Crash. It's for my child. *Our* child. We'll both need you."

"Cordelia, no."

"You have to help me," she rushed on. "I don't know how to be a parent, and I don't want to mess this up, Crash. I need you to show me."

"But you've got your family and unlimited resources to make—"

"But I need *you*, Crash. Don't you see? I love you!"

The worlds almost bowled him over. Cordelia's earnest face told him he hadn't heard wrong.

"You care for me, too," she went on. "You don't have to say it. I know you well enough now. You care about this baby, and you care about me."

Crash couldn't help himself. He kissed her. He loved the way her arms slipped around his neck as she responded to his lips on hers. She made a joyful sound in the back of her throat. By God, he *did* care about this wild, passionate woman. All his good sense evaporated in the heat of her embrace. Crash gathered her close and longed to bury himself inside her warmth.

"I couldn't let you go," she said, feverishly kissing his face. "I had to come after you. And Rudi—"

"I thought Rudi hated my guts."

"He doesn't. He worries about me. But something changed his mind. I think he would have suggested I come even if I hadn't gone to him first."

"But—"

"Don't argue with me, Crash. Just kiss me. Hold me. Make love to me."

Crash had already peeled off her sweater—a light garment that was far too thin to keep her warm. Her skin broke into a rash of goose bumps beneath his hands. Suddenly she was shivering in his arms. Frowning, Crash pulled Cordelia to the bed with the plan of warming her beneath the covers. "Take it easy, love."

"Crash, make love with me."

"Let's just get you warm first, all right? Princess, you're shaking like a leaf."

"I was so afraid," she admitted, voice quivering as he pressed her down into the bedclothes. "I was afraid of losing you, of being alone. While I hid in here, I started to get afraid you'd be angry—"

"I'm not angry. I'm worried."

He was, too. Holding Cordelia, Crash could feel how upset she had become. Her heart felt as if it were beating at double its normal rhythm. To soothe her, he slid into the bed and pulled Cordelia close again, cradling her quaking body against his own.

"Oh, Crash," she said, then hiccuped. "I'm not the weepy type. I don't know what's wrong with me. I can't think straight."

"It's okay. You don't have to think now. Just relax."

"I had to get away. Papa said—"

"Shh. I don't need to hear what Papa had to say. Not now. Be quiet."

"You—you're so kind—especially when I'm acting like an idiot."

"You're not an idiot. At least, not all the time."

"Thanks," she said, then laughed. "I plead temporary insanity."

"It's understandable." Crash stroked her hair and felt the tension begin to ease its way out of her. "You've had a rough couple of days. And last night—"

"Last night was wonderful," she said softly. "Magical."

Crash kissed the top of her head. "I thought so, too."

"Now, though—I don't know what's wrong with me."

"You're just upset."

"No," she said, her voice changing suddenly. "It's not that. I feel strange." She trailed one hand down her side until she reached the distended curve of her belly. The rest of her body went still. Very still. For a long moment she did not speak.

"What's wrong?" Crash demanded, suddenly alarmed by her silence. "Princess—"

"Oh, dear," she whispered.

She put both hands on her belly.

Suddenly a huge gush of water flooded the bedclothes, thoroughly soaking the sheets and Cordelia's clothing. She sat up with a cry.

Crash choked. "The baby's coming? *Now?*"

It took every iota of Crash's strength not to leap out of the bed and go looking for the nearest parachute. Suddenly he'd rather be free-falling through the atmosphere than staying in that cabin with a woman on the brink of delivering a baby. A real *baby*. A thousand emotions exploded in his brain—fear, desperation, excitement, and mostly terror. "But...but—you c-can't!" he sputtered. "Not here! We're thousands of feet above the Atlantic!"

"I can't help it," Cordelia said, sounding utterly calm and awestruck at the same time by the powerful sensations that had begun to take control of her body. She smoothed her hands around the mound of her belly as if hypnotized.

Crash scrambled up on his knees and grabbed Cordelia's wrists. Gripping her hard, he forced her to look him directly in the eyes. She blinked, as if mystified by her predicament, and appeared unable to focus on anything else.

Speaking distinctly, Crash said, "Listen to me, Cordelia. We're a long way from civilization. Unless the steward knows something about delivering babies, you've got to hang on until we get back to Cordofino."

Cordelia swallowed hard. "I—I don't think I'm going to have any say in the matter, Crash."

"Damn," he growled, plumping the pillows and settling her back against the soft cushion. He ripped back the sodden sheets and dumped them on the floor. "You got yourself worked into hysterics and now this—!"

"I can't help it," she repeated, voice dreamy. "The baby's coming."

"Are you sure?"

She nodded and went on staring at her belly. "I felt everything inside get tight. Even in my back and down my legs. Then it went away and came back again. Those are labor contractions, aren't they? My doctor's nurse once showed me a film—"

Panic closed Crash's throat for one awful instant. "That's all you know about childbirth? What you saw in one lousy film?"

She looked up then, and anger flashed in her eyes. "I thought I'd have enough time to get ready!" she said defensively. "And I thought I'd have plenty of doctors around when I needed them!"

"Well, now it's you and me, Princess," said Crash, making her comfortable in the bed. "Just you and me together."

Cordelia reached for his hand and stopped him. She looked up at him and managed an unsteady smile that made his heart lurch. Softly she said, "I wouldn't have it any other way, Crash."

Ten

Rudi, hiding out in the steward's closet, was horrified to learn that Princess Cordelia had gone into labor. "But...but—this cannot be!"

"Oh, yes it can, pal," Crash told him, then outlined the whole situation. "Do you know anything about babies?"

"They smell," said Rudi.

"That's a big help!"

"Well, it's the extent of my expertise."

"What about childbirth?"

"What about it? You mean—? Oh, no. I can't do it! I'm her bodyguard, not her...her—"

"I'll go talk to the pilot. You look around for some supplies."

"What kind of supplies?"

"Baby-delivering supplies!"

"What would that be, exactly?"

"How should I know? Just look around!"

Crash made his way to the cockpit of the jet, where he met equal quantities of horror and amusement from the rest of the crew.

The pilot—the most levelheaded of the three men in the cockpit—picked up the telephone at once and solemnly communicated Cordelia's escape to the palace. Then he spoke with a series of airports while the navigator calculated the fastest way to reach a hospital.

The final report was not what Crash wanted to hear.

"With the Canary Islands socked in with high winds, we're an hour from the next nearest hospital," the young navigator said, "which is an American air force base in Iceland."

"*Iceland?* What about getting to the States?"

The navigator shook his head. "That's even farther away, I'm afraid."

"Can we go back to Cordofino?"

"It will be faster to go to Iceland. How far apart are Her Royal Highness's contractions?"

The question rang a bell in Crash's mind. Somehow, he knew that information was important. "I don't know how far apart they are," he admitted. "Should I go time them?"

The navigator slid his headset off his tousled blond hair and looked up at Crash with clear brown eyes. "If you do, we'll have a better idea of how much time we've got."

"Hey," Crash said, grabbing the man's arm. "You sound like you know something about delivering babies."

"Just what I see in the movies, I'm afraid. I faint at the sight of blood."

"We may need your help, just the same."

"Oh, I couldn't—"

"You may not have a choice."

The pilot interrupted. "Listen, having a baby can take hours," he remarked over his shoulder. "My sister took days. We'll be landing in plenty of time. Until then, keep Her Highness comfortable."

Comfortable. Sounded easy enough. But somehow Crash knew it wasn't going to be the least bit easy.

The copilot was laughing. "Just keep her from screaming too loud, will you?"

Shakily making his way back to Cordelia's private cabin, Crash noted that Rudi had disappeared. Grimly, Crash wondered if the bodyguard had escaped by jumping into the ocean.

Crash pounded on the door to the steward's closet. "Hey, Rudi, you better not be hiding in there!"

"Go away!"

"I wish I could," Crash growled. "But I can't, and you're stuck, too. Bring us some extra towels and sheets. And a pitcher of water!"

"But—but—"

"Do it!"

Rudi began making a noise that sounded suspiciously like whimpering, but Crash could hear him rummaging in cupboards and knew he'd started to obey orders.

"Crash!"

Cordelia's voice, coming down the passageway— sounded strangled, so Crash hurried away from Rudi and let himself into her cabin.

"Oh, Crash," she said, gasping for breath. "I thought you'd never get back!"

"I'm here, I'm here."

She fell back against the pillows, brushing long strands of hair away from her shining forehead. Clearly she'd just experienced a powerful contraction and looked anything but comfortable. But during his absence she had also managed to change out of her soaked clothing into a loosely flowing nightgown. Trust Cordelia to look beautiful while going through labor. She was panting as if she'd run a mile.

Crash sat on the edge of the bed and reached for her hands. "Tell me what's happening."

"The baby's definitely coming." She caught her breath at last. "These aren't practice contractions."

"How far apart are they?"

She frowned. "I don't know. A few minutes, that's all."

"Twenty minutes? Ten minutes?"

"Oh, no, much closer than that. Five or less."

Crash suppressed the urge to groan. He wanted to shout at her—tell her to stop misbehaving immediately. But he knew she couldn't control what was happening.

She used a clip to pull her hair into a ponytail. "How long will it take to get back to Cordofino?"

Too long, Crash almost said. But he bit down on the words and managed a smile instead. No sense terrifying them both. To give himself time to think, he tucked a few loose tendrils of Cordelia's hair behind her ears. "The pilot thinks we're better off heading for someplace closer."

"France? England? I know a wonderful doctor in London. He collects fountain pens, I think."

"Fountain pens." Crash decided not to mention that the next doctor to enter Cordelia's life was likely to be an American air force officer who was probably annoyed as hell about getting stuck in Iceland and was hardly qualified to take care of a delicate royal princess. "Well, let's just see what the pilot can manage, shall we? You and I will concentrate on keeping you comfortable."

"I'm not the least comfortable, Crash. My back is killing me. But that's to be expected, I guess. Look what I found!" She pulled a large card out from under the bedclothes. "It was in the first-aid kit! It's a brochure about delivering babies!"

She unfolded the card, and it was printed with drawings and brief instructions. One look at the pictures made Crash's head swim.

But Cordelia didn't notice. She went on happily, "I skimmed through it while you were gone. It sounds relatively simple. I think I'm in transition labor right now. See? This is where the baby is."

Rather than look at the place she pointed to on the card, Crash closed his eyes to hold back a wave of dizziness.

"I'm supposed to walk around as long as I can, to help the baby thin out my cervix."

"Thin out your—"

"Never mind. Just help me up."

Crash did as he was told. Once on her feet, Cordelia swayed and rubbed the small of her back. "God," she grumbled. "This is annoying."

"Are you in pain?"

"No, it's just an ache."

Cordelia looked up and finally noticed the worry flickering in Crash's face. He'd gone very pale. Bravely, she grinned. "Hey, I'm the one having this baby, you know."

"Yes, but—well, I don't want you to suffer."

Her heart went out to him, but she managed a laugh. "Suffer! Crash, I'm in perfect health. And I'm good with pain. Honest. Once I fractured my leg in a skiing accident and I never broke a sweat."

"This is different."

"I'll be okay." She patted his chest. "I planned to miss out on this and enjoy a nice drug-induced sleep instead, but I'll handle it."

Crash looked doubtful.

"Hey, my family has a history of short labors. Despite my mother's claims to being royalty since the beginning of civilization, we have the disgustingly peasantlike ability to drop our children in the field and keep working."

"What can I do to help?"

"Walk me around. The baby will come faster if I stay on my feet."

"Then sit down immediately!"

"Crash!"

"I mean it!" he roared. "We don't want this happening any sooner than we can help it!"

"Are you kidding? I want this over with!"

"Quit being so stubborn. Sit down and wait, for crying out loud! Do you want to have our baby over the Atlantic?"

"I want to get rid of this backache," she snapped back. "So if you'll just— You know, that's the first time you've ever called it *our* baby."

"Well, it's true."

"I know, but— Oh. Ow! Oh, brother, here it comes again!"

The wave of pressure hit Cordelia in the belly and made her stagger back toward the bed. Crash eased her down, murmuring something soothing, but Cordelia was suddenly deaf to his words. Instead she found herself listening to her own body. Every nerve and powerful sinew seemed to tighten and focus on the task at hand. She shut out the whole world and turned inward.

Then she became dimly aware of Crash's voice.

"You're turning blue, you're turning blue," he seemed to be chanting frantically as he leaned over her and held on to her shoulders, shaking them. "Breathe, Princess. For God's sake, breathe!"

"I—I'm—sup-supposed to—to p-p-pant!"

"Then pant! Don't hold your breath!"

Breathing seemed to make the pressure worse, but when Cordelia quit sucking in great gulps of breath and started to pant in a shallow rhythm, she suddenly felt in better control. "I—"

"Don't talk," Crash ordered. "Just pant. It'll be over in a few seconds. That's it, that's it. Good girl."

The door of the cabin opened at that moment, and Rudi came stumbling into Cordelia's room. The big man's arms were full of linens and a silver pitcher of water, which he promptly spilled on the carpet. He gave a croaking cry and stared at Cordelia as if she'd suddenly grown two heads.

"Shut up!" Crash roared at Rudi. "Can't you see she needs help?"

But Cordelia didn't feel as if she needed help. Instead she felt an overwhelming sense of calm settle over herself. Suddenly she was surrounded by an aura of purpose and determination. She concentrated on panting and closed her eyes while Crash went over and wrestled the linens away from Rudi. She was vaguely aware that Rudi could not budge his feet from the spot where he was frozen.

When the contraction passed, she opened her eyes. Crash and Rudi were arguing hotly.

"Stop it!" Cordelia cried. "Stop, the both of you!"

"Your Highness, my job description doesn't include anything like this," Rudi began feverishly. "And I—"

"And you're squeamish," Crash accused.

"I am not!'

"You are, too!"

"I feel sick!" Rudi cried. "I can't help it. My stomach hurts."

As if to prove his point, Rudi suddenly doubled over with pain.

"What in the world?" Crash looked disgusted as he towered over Rudi. "What's the matter with you? Two minutes ago, you were healthy as an ox!"

"Well, I'm not now!" Rudi gasped. "It hurts!"

"I'll show you something that hurts," Crash shouted, lifting his fist.

"Crash! Crash, stop it!" Cordelia struggled up from the bed in time to grab Crash's arm before he punched the helpless Rudi. She hung on, saying, "He can't help the way he feels. It's probably sympathetic labor pains."

"Are you kidding? What baloney!"

"Here, help me get Rudi onto the bed."

"The hell he's going into your bed! Oh, hell, we'll put him in the chair over there."

Together, Crash and Cordelia lowered the groaning Rudi into a plush slipper chair. There the bodyguard slumped backward and clutched his stomach. His face turned a sickly green color, and he squeezed his eyes shut tight. The room suddenly rang with his groans.

"I don't believe this." Crash was incredulous. "What kind of bodyguard is that?"

"A good one," Cordelia replied, tucking a small pillow behind Rudi's head. "And a wonderful friend."

"Are you sure you want this wonderful friend here when you give birth?"

"Well," she said doubtfully, glancing at the miserable Rudi. "I hate to move him now. Let's give him some time to calm down."

"Time!" Crash exclaimed, hastily checking his watch. "I was supposed to time your contractions. Sit down, sit down, will you?"

"I'd rather stand."

"Princess, can't I convince you to slow this process down just long enough to get to a hospital?"

"I'm fine. Nothing's going to go wrong. Just let me— Oh, oh! Here it comes again."

The force of her next contraction threw Cordelia onto the bed. She gasped and panted, but it was no use. This time the contraction got out of control. Blindly, Cordelia grabbed for something to hang on to and found herself gripping Crash's forearm.

"Breathe!" he coached, climbing onto the bed with her.

"I'm *trying!*"

Rudi groaned.

Cordelia panted.

Crash cursed.

Then the door opened and a fair-haired young man entered the cabin. "Can I . . . ?"

"Who are you?" Cordelia practically growled, not recognizing the stranger.

"The plane's navigator," Crash supplied, wrapping his free arm around Cordelia's shoulders. "He'll help us. Won't you pal? Help me get the princess comfortable. We need those pillows—"

But the navigator was no help at all. He took a long look at Cordelia and turned pale. Then his eyes rolled up in his head and he fainted, falling across the carpet with a muffled thud.

"Great," muttered Crash.

He got up and rolled the navigator out into the passageway. With a little more gentleness, he manhandled Rudi out, too, leaving the two of them alone in the cabin.

For the next half hour, Cordelia felt as if she had been transported to another dimension. Her body became something completely foreign and unattached. Every few minutes her belly hardened, her muscles turned hot and she heard her own voice tear out of her throat like the cry of a wild animal. It was hard work such as she'd never known—exhausting, excruciating labor.

Eventually she felt an overwhelming urge quite unlike anything she'd ever expected.

"I've got to push," she told Crash, who had braced her against the headboard and had stuck to her side every minute.

"My God, we must almost be to an airport—"

"I can't stop, Crash." She reached for both his hands and met his determined gaze with her own. "It's just you and me here, but we've got to do this now."

"You and me? Now?"

A wild laugh bubbled up from inside her. "Maybe you weren't there for the conception, but you're here for the baby's birth. Oh, Crash! I'm so sorry!"

"Sorry?" He matched her laugh with an incredulous one of his own. "For what?"

"Getting you into this. Coming up with this whole harebrained idea. Dragging you around the world and then sticking you with the job of delivering the baby you should never have known about—"

"My love," he said, silencing her by cupping her damp face in his hand. Crash smiled deeply into her eyes. "I wouldn't have missed this for anything."

Cordelia smiled as Crash eased down to kiss her fully on the mouth. His lips tasted salty and firm, and his warmth and reassurance filled her with renewed strength. Cordelia found herself blinking back tears when they parted and gazed into each other's souls for a long, magical moment.

"I love you," Crash whispered.

"Oh, Crash. I love you, too. You are nobler than any polo-playing prince. You have more courage than any blue-blooded twit in Europe. I love you so much!"

He laughed. "How did this happen?"

"It's crazy."

"It's wonderful."

"A miracle." Cordelia sighed, touching his face with trembling fingertips.

Crash's hand rested on her belly, and he felt the muscles tighten there at the same moment Cordelia did. Gently he said, "I think it's time for another miracle."

"Y-yes."

"Ready to give me your baby, Princess?"

"Our baby, my love."

Then the magic seemed to suspend time. Cordelia wasn't sure if minutes passed or hours. She remembered no pain—at least none she'd ever known before—just a tremendous surge of power beyond anything she could imagine. Suddenly she was stronger than any being on earth. She heard Crash's voice, steady and unwavering as she pushed. She felt his hands and the touch of his lips on her face, her breasts, her belly as she worked to deliver his child. And when he received the baby from her, he did it as gently as if he'd been making love to her for hours.

Cordelia wept, and her tears mingled with his as they cradled the small living creature together on the bed. All as the jet shot through the clouds and headed for earth . . . and reality.

Eleven

"Is it a boy or a girl?" Princess Geraldine could hardly contain her excitement and pranced around clapping her hands. "Can I hold him—or her? Which *is* it? Heavens, Cordelia, why must you be so secretive?"

"Because Papa said you don't intend to recognize this child, Mama. As far as you're concerned, he doesn't exist!"

"A boy!" Geraldine cried, stretching out her hands to the small bundle Cordelia cradled in her arms. "Oh, how I wanted a little boy! After all you girls it would have been a nice change, but your father never— Oh, *please,* can't I hold him? Charles, make her give my grandson to me!"

Crash grinned around the stub of a fine cigar—one of many he'd purchased at the air force base exchange in Iceland. "Let her hold the baby, Princess."

"Why should I?" Cordelia demanded, her eyes sparking with anger that Crash knew was completely feigned. In her heart she was enormously proud of her son and never missed a chance to show him off.

"Because your mother wants to hold her first grandchild."

"I don't want to give him up."

"What a change of heart!" Geraldine cried. "I seem to remember hearing you intended to hire round-the-clock nannies to take care of your baby. You couldn't be bothered with motherhood!"

Cordelia smiled up at Crash. "I couldn't bear the thought of anyone else looking after him now. Here, Mama. Meet our son."

"Oh, you little darling!" Princess Geraldine enveloped the baby with delighted coos and quickly carried him to the French window to make a fuss over him. The last rays of Cordofinian sunset cast a golden halo around the baby's tiny head.

Cordelia took off her jacket and perched on the arm of one of the sofas in her living quarters at the Cordofino palace. She smiled as she watched her mother hold the baby. Looking down at her, Crash marveled at her beauty. She had been amazing when she was pregnant, but now he was just beginning to see what a magnificent woman she was. In a new pair of American-made blue jeans and an air force sweatshirt, she looked as delectable as a college coed on spring break.

He puffed on his cigar and stretched contentedly. After three weeks in Iceland, Crash was glad to be back in the lap of luxury. Although they'd been made welcome and comfortable at the air force base with their newborn, both Crash and Cordelia had felt the need to get back to the real world. They had been relieved when the American doctor finally gave them permission to take the baby on a pressurized flight off the frozen island.

The royal summons from Cordofino had come the same day. Cordelia hadn't been inclined to acknowledge her father's command to return to the palace for a visit, but Crash had persuaded her to go back to find out what her family wanted to discuss.

After all, she was a princess by birth. What kind of life would they have living his reckless life-style? Crash thought she needed one more glimpse of palace life before she gave it all up for freedom.

"I can't go without you," Cordelia had said that night in the hospital, where she'd stayed to be near the baby. "I never want to go anywhere without you again, Crash."

And Crash had known he couldn't leave her, either. Somehow, fate had drawn them together. Nothing short of death was ever going to part them. "Go back one more time," he had encouraged her. "Just to show off our son."

The idea was irresistible to her, so they had come.

At the window, Geraldine turned. "What's his name? You've given him a name, haven't you?"

"Of course, Mama. He's Alexander Henri Phillippe Craddock."

Geraldine smiled down at her grandson. "Alexander. What a big name for such a little boy!"

"He'll grow into it," Crash said confidently.

"Why, Charles, I believe he has your eyes."

"And Cordelia's nose."

At that moment Rudi entered the suite of rooms, lugging a large plastic diaper bag over his shoulder.

The bag was clearly printed with the words It's A Boy! Rudi seemed uneasy carrying the item, but he managed to appear dignified as he placed it on the sofa next to Cordelia.

"Oh, thanks, Rudi. Did you find everything?"

"The disposables with the reusable tapes, Your Highness, yes."

"And a binky?"

Rudi didn't flinch. "Yes, Your Highness, I found another binky."

"Thanks, Rudi, you're a treasure."

Rudi remained stone-faced.

Geraldine fluttered back from the window, carrying the baby. "May I take him downstairs? Your sisters are dying to see him, Cordelia, and although your father pretends to be completely unmoved by your return, I know he's itching to get his hands on another little one!"

"Papa likes babies?"

"Darling, he adores them! Why, he used to hold you for hours while you napped! He even took you to meetings and carried you shamelessly around the stables."

Cordelia looked astonished. "He did?"

"Of course, dear. It's when you started to talk that he became unnerved by you."

"Papa—unnerved?" Cordelia blinked. "That's hard to believe."

"May I take Alexander downstairs, Charles?"

With a grin, Crash said, "Sure, Mama. Take Rudi along to change the diapers, though. He needs the practice."

Rudi gave Crash a withering glance but obediently followed Geraldine from the apartment.

When they were alone, Cordelia arose from the sofa and removed the cigar from Crash's mouth. Tossing it into an ashtray, she put her arms around Crash's neck and smiled up at him. "Thank you for making me come home. I want everybody to see what a beautiful child we made."

"He is a handsome little guy, isn't he?"

"Of course. He looks just like his father."

Crash wrapped his arms around Cordelia's newly slender body and pulled her close. Huskily he said, "If he's half as good-looking as his mother, he'll be a devil with the rest of his kindergarten class in a few years. You look beautiful in this light, Princess."

Her smile reached all the way to her eyes, and they glimmered with love. "I'm glad we had some time alone together, Crash."

"Alone? You call three weeks hanging around a hospital being alone?"

"I mean away from my family. It's given us time to know each other better."

"Do you like what you've gotten to know?"

"I love it," she whispered, lifting her mouth to kiss him. "I love you."

She pressed her lips softly against Crash's, and the contact suddenly sent his brain into a spin. She smelled delicious, felt lithe and slim in his arms, and she tasted warm and willing on his lips. Crash gathered her close until their bodies melted together. Desire shot through him, hot and tingling.

Cordelia must have felt the same frisson of electricity. She opened her eyes and smiled up at him. "We really are alone this time, aren't we?"

"Completely."

"Exciting, isn't it?"

"Very."

"Crash—"

He kissed her deeply this time and enjoyed the un-steady sigh she gave as their tongues met shyly at first, then more sensually. Cordelia pressed closer, and the fullness of her breasts sent shivers of pleasure down Crash's body. He passed a caress down the curve of her hips and nuzzled her throat. "Princess—"

"Oh, yes, please," she whispered.

"It's not too soon?"

"Not soon enough," she responded, taking his hand in hers and drawing Crash toward her bedroom.

He undressed her slowly, taking pleasure in discovering the new shape of her body. He covered her satiny skin with kisses and laughed when she gave up struggling with the snap on his jeans and begged him to undress quickly. Then they were naked together in the soft bedclothes and wrapped in each other's arms, warm and breathless.

"God, Princess, I do love you." Crash pinned her to the bed and settled gently against the tautness of her curves.

"I'm so glad." Her gaze shone in the dusky light of early evening.

"Sometimes I wish I could feel differently—"

"No, Crash."

"I can't help thinking I'm ruining your life."

"No. You've opened the whole world to me."

"But you're sacrificing everything—"

"For love. For a child. For my freedom." Cordelia pulled him down, opening herself to Crash and drawing him into her heart. "You've given me all those things, Crash. And I love you for them all."

He groaned and sank slowly inside her. She felt gloriously sensual, and she was his, *his.* He claimed her gently, delighted she was so ready for him.

"My love," she whispered, holding his head against her breast. He could feel the flutter of her pulse and the soft gasp of her breath as he moved within her.

Cordelia sighed. She caressed him everywhere, tracing her fingertips, then her lips along the strong lines of his shoulders, his jaw, his face. She arched delicately against him at first, then with increasing passion.

At last she cried out in wonderment, pulsing with pleasure, and Crash heard himself give an answering moan. Locked in that explosive union, he told her again and again. He loved her. More than life. More than anything.

Later, there was time for playfulness. Time for exploring and gentle kisses. Time for laughter and the savoring of desire. More than once, Crash felt his eyes sting with simple, joyful happiness.

No one came bursting in on their private hours. But at last the bedside telephone gave a tiny squeak, rousing Cordelia from drowsily caressing Crash's bare chest. She reached across him and picked up the receiver.

"Yes, Mama," she murmured when a voice on the other end began to chatter. "All right, if you think it's important. Yes, in a few minutes."

She handed the receiver to Crash, who cradled it again. Then he asked, "What was that?"

"A summons to the throne room."

"Oh, damn. Do we have to go?"

Cordelia was frowning. "She said it was important. And from the tone of her voice...well, something's happening, Crash."

"Is Alexander all right?"

"He's fine. Sleeping peacefully at the moment. But I think we'd better get dressed and go downstairs." She kissed him once more and then rolled over. "You know, I'm going to enjoy living someplace where I won't get called on the carpet every day."

Crash didn't answer, but lay pensively in the bed while she sauntered into the bathroom and turned on the shower.

Cordelia showered and then dressed in her jeans once again while Crash got cleaned up. She was brushing out her hair when he emerged from the shower and climbed into his clothes. But then he took the hairbrush from her hands and finished the job himself, watching her eyes in the mirror as he stroked her hair. She sensed he had something important on his mind.

"Princess," he said at last. "I want you to be happy."

She covered his hand where it rested on her shoulder. "I know."

"So if your family wants to take you back, I think—"

"That argument is over, Crash."

"But you belong here. In comfort. Where there's important work to do. Where—"

"I belong with you and Alexander. Please, Crash. I know my own heart."

"I think I know it, too. You may need some time to kick up your heels, but your whole life has been in training, Princess, for a kind of destiny that doesn't come to many people on this earth. I think your father's right. You were brought up to this. To more than I can give you."

"Don't say that." Cordelia got up quickly. "I won't listen to any more talk like that."

"You know it's true, though."

"Let's go downstairs."

Crash didn't argue further. He took her hand in his, though, as they descended the staircase together, and Cordelia's heart swelled with love for him.

In the throne room Cordelia was surprised to see the whole family assembled without a single servant in sight. Her sisters Julianna and Angelique were giggling over the tiny bundle of Alexander, while Princess Geraldine sat smiling, on the gilded chair beside Cordelia's father. On his throne Prince Henri looked aloof as ever, but Cordelia thought she saw a gleam of pleasure in his gaze as he watched her enter.

"Hello, Papa," Cordelia said, stopping before the throne.

"Hello, Cordelia." The prince's words contained a raspy note as he addressed her. He could not keep his affection a secret. Then his eyes turned to Crash, and he said formally, "Hello, Mr., uh, Craddock."

Crash noted the prince's acknowledgment with a surprisingly well-executed bow.

"I am happy," said the prince, "to see that you are in good health, Cordelia."

"Thank you, Papa."

"And your son is remarkably handsome for his age."

Cordelia smiled and hoped her lips didn't tremble. "Good genes, Papa."

The prince lifted one eyebrow. "Better genes than we first imagined, I understand."

"What?"

Crash stiffened by Cordelia's side.

Princess Geraldine leaned forward. "It was very naughty of you, Charles, to keep such a secret."

"What secret?" Cordelia blurted, suddenly aware that she was the only one in the room who didn't know what was going on. Even Crash seemed suddenly uneasy.

"It seems Mr. Craddock," said the prince, "is not who he claims to be."

"He doesn't claim to be anybody!" Cordelia snapped.

"Now, now, Princess, let's not let your temper get out of hand."

Cordelia swung on Crash. "My temper is just fine! They're going to play some kind of trick on us, Crash. I should have known—"

"The only trick," said the prince, "was played by your, uh, Mr. Craddock. If that's his real name."

"What do you mean?" Bewildered, Cordelia looked at her father, then her mother. "What's going on, Mama?"

Princess Geraldine was smiling. "Ask Charles, dear. I think he has something to tell you."

"Something to tell me?"

"Or would you rather we break the news, Charles?"

Crash glowered at Cordelia's mother. "How did you find out?"

Geraldine laughed delightedly. "I have my sources, dear boy! And from the little clues you dropped, I had enough information to organize a thorough search."

"A search of what?" Cordelia demanded.

"His background, dear. Shall I tell her, Charles?"

"No," said Crash. "I never wanted—" He turned to Cordelia, his face twisted with indecision. "This wasn't supposed to happen, Princess. I made my choice long ago."

"What choice? Will somebody *please* tell me what's going on?"

"I'm not an American," Crash said unwillingly. He took Cordelia's hands in his and held her fast. "I emigrated to the United States with my mother when I was six years old."

"So?"

"We came from a small country, Cordelia. Bonifria. It doesn't exist anymore, but it was near Greece. It was swallowed after World War II, divided between several Baltic countries."

"I—I don't understand."

"The history doesn't matter," Crash said quickly. "I went to the States and tried to forget who I was. After the war, when things were so bad for my family, my mother insisted we start anew. She was so much like you, Cordelia. You'd have loved her. She wanted to be free. She hated the tragedy of—well, everything that happened to the family. She wanted me to have the kind of life she didn't."

"What kind of life are you talking about? Crash, please—"

"She married into the royal family of Bonifria," Crash said quickly. "She came from France—from a very good family. And my father—my father was Prince Alexander of Bonifria. That's why I wanted our son to have his name. But I—"

Cordelia stared at him. "You're the son of a royal prince?"

"Yes," Crash said at last.

Holding Alexander, Angelique began to laugh. "Good heavens, he's Prince *Charles!*"

Cordelia stared at Crash, unable to process the information he had just revealed. "No," she said softly. "I don't believe this. I can't—I— *Why?* Why did you do it?"

"Keep my identity a secret? Who would care? I wasn't a prince anymore. When my mother and I traveled to the States, we had very little money. Eventually, she worked, but we were always poor. Then I went to live in Texas and—well, have you any idea what Texans would do to somebody who claimed to be a royal prince?"

"But, Crash—"

"My past never mattered. It was the present my mother always wanted me to live for."

"But—but—"

"Yes, I'm a prince."

"A prince," Cordelia repeated, too stunned to say more.

Geraldine and Prince Henri stepped down from their thrones and formally greeted Crash. Their bows and firm handshakes were more than a welcome of one head of state to another. It was a welcome into a family.

Dazed, Cordelia said, "A prince. I'm in love with a prince, after all."

"We'd be delighted," said Prince Henri, "to make you a part of our family, Charles. And someday, I hope you'll help Cordelia look after this country of ours."

"But—but—" Cordelia couldn't make the words come out without difficulty. "Papa, that damned law needs to be changed! I shouldn't have to marry a prince! I should be allowed to marry whomever I choose!''

"And whom," asked Crash laughingly, "do you choose?"

"You shouldn't have to *be* a prince!"

Prince Henri said, "When you sit on the throne of Cordofino, my dear Cordelia, you may change any law you choose to change. But in the meantime, young lady, you're going to marry a prince!"

"Yes," said Crash, gathering Cordelia into his arms for a kiss. "You're going to marry a prince. And we're going to have lots of little princes, too."

"Amazing," said Cordelia.

* * * * *

Get Ready to be Swept Away by
Silhouette's Spring Collection

Abduction *&* Seduction

These passion-filled stories explore both the dangerous
desires of men and the seductive powers of women.
Written by three of our most celebrated authors, they are
sure to capture your hearts.

Diana Palmer
Brings us a spin-off of her Long, Tall Texans series

Joan Johnston
Crafts a beguiling Western romance

Rebecca Brandewyne
New York Times bestselling author
makes a smashing contemporary debut

Available in March at your favorite retail outlet.

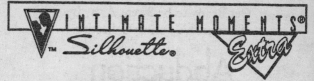

You won't want to miss...

by Merline Lovelace

Starting in May 1995, Merline Lovelace brings her
new miniseries, CODE NAME: DANGER, to Silhouette
Intimate Moments. And the first title, *Night of the Jaguar*
(IM #637), is also an INTIMATE MOMENTS EXTRA.

Alias: Jaguar. *Agency:* OMEGA. Secret Agent
Jake MacKenzie hadn't planned on rescuing
Sarah Chandler and three frightened children from
the jungles of Central America. Then a drug bust
gone awry made him an unwilling savior—
and all-too-willing lover.

Coming your way in August 1995 is
The Cowboy and the Cossack (IM #657).

Join the excitement of Merline Lovelace's
CODE NAME: DANGER, as the daring men and
women who comprise the Omega Agency find love
despite the most perilous odds, only in—

COMING NEXT MONTH FROM

SILHOUETTE®

Desire®

The next installment of the delightful

HAZARDS INC. series

THE MADDENING MODEL
by
SUZANNE SIMMS

Sunday Harrington was beautiful, brainy...and Simon
Hazard found her unbearable—until the pair got stranded in
the jungle and he learned that there was more to her than
met the eye.

HAZARDS, INC.: Danger is their business; love is
their reward!

HAZ

And now for something completely different...

SILHOUETTE® *Desire*

MAN of the Month

1995

Don't let the winter months get you down because the heat is about to get turned way up...with the sexiest hunks of 1995!

January: **A NUISANCE**
by Lass Small

February: **COWBOYS DON'T CRY**
by Anne McAllister

March: **THAT BURKE MAN**
the 75th Man of the Month
by Diana Palmer

April: **MR. EASY**
by Cait London

May: **MYSTERIOUS MOUNTAIN MAN**
by Annette Broadrick

June: **SINGLE DAD**
by Jennifer Greene

**MAN OF THE MONTH...
ONLY FROM
SIILHOUETTE DESIRE**

MOM95JJ-R

is
DIANA PALMER'S
THAT BURKE MAN

He's rugged, lean and determined. He's a
Long, Tall Texan. His name is Burke, and he's
March's *Man of the Month*—Silhouette Desire's
75th!

Meet this sexy cowboy in Diana Palmer's
THAT BURKE MAN, available in March 1995!

Man of the Month...only from Silhouette Desire!